Love, Italian-style!

Welcome to Venice. We promise you will never be bored! Why, you could even fall in love. But make sure your new *amore* is not promised to another and leaves you at the altar. Of course, if that does happen, a handsome duke could come to your rescue and give you a job. Just remember to tell your family about your change in plans before they come to visit. Otherwise they may think your handsome duke boss is your new fiancé and you two would have to pretend to be engaged for their sake. Then again, you may find that the magic of our Italian moon brings you and your boss even closer together...!

Dear Reader,

Though each Special Edition novel is sprinkled with magic, you should know that the authors of your favorite romances are *not* magicians—they're women just like you.

"Romance is a refuge for me. It lifts my spirits." Sound familiar? That's Christine Rimmer's answer to why she reads—and writes—romance. Christine is the author of this month's *The Tycoon's Instant Daughter,* which launches our newest in-line continuity the STOCKWELLS OF TEXAS. Like you, she started out as a reader while she had a multifaceted career—actress, janitor, waitress, phone sales representative. "But I really wanted one job where I wouldn't have to work any other jobs," Christine recalls. Now, thirteen years and thirty-seven books later, Ms. Rimmer is an established voice in Special Edition.

Some other wonderful voices appear this month. Susan Mallery delivers *Unexpectedly Expecting!,* the latest in her LONE STAR CANYON series. Penny Richards's juicy series RUMOR HAS IT... continues with *Judging Justine.* It's love Italian-style with Tracy Sinclair's *Pretend Engagement,* an alluring romance set in Venice. The cat is out of the bag, so to speak, in Diana Whitney's *The Not-So-Secret Baby.* And young Trent Brody is hoping to see his *Beloved Bachelor Dad* happily married in Crystal Green's debut novel.

We aim to give you six novels every month that lift *your* spirits. Tell me what you like about Special Edition. What would you like to see more of in the line? Write to: Silhouette Books, 300 East 42nd St., 6th Floor, New York, NY 10017. I encourage you to be part of making your favorite line even better!

Best,

Karen Taylor Richman
Senior Editor

Please address questions and book requests to:
Silhouette Reader Service
U.S.: 3010 Walden Ave., P.O. Box 1325, Buffalo, NY 14269
Canadian: P.O. Box 609, Fort Erie, Ont. L2A 5X3

Pretend Engagement

TRACY SINCLAIR

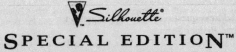

SPECIAL EDITION™

Published by Silhouette Books

America's Publisher of Contemporary Romance

For Ed, my inspiration and my best friend.

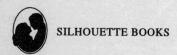 SILHOUETTE BOOKS

ISBN 0-373-24372-3

PRETEND ENGAGEMENT

Visit Silhouette at www.eHarlequin.com

Printed in U.S.A.

Books by Tracy Sinclair

TRACY SINCLAIR

began her career as a photojournalist for national magazines and newspapers. Extensive travel all over the world has provided this California resident with countless fascinating experiences, settings and acquaintances to draw on in plotting her romances. After writing over fifty novels for Silhouette, she still has stories she can't wait to tell.

Chapter One

"Do you take this man to be your lawful wedded husband?"

A shiver ran down Jillian Colby's spine as she listened to the solemn words that would bind her forever to Rinaldo Marsala, a man she hardly knew. Was she making a terrible mistake?

Rinaldo nudged her gently, and she realized that he and the priest were waiting for her answer. How could she back out now, literally at the last minute? She glanced around, seeking some escape, any reason for not going through with the ceremony.

The ancient church on one of Venice's smaller canals was almost empty. Jillian didn't know anyone else in Venice, and Rinaldo hadn't invited either his family or friends to the wedding. There were only a few people who had wandered in early for the evening services. One of them was a young woman with a baby in her arms. Jillian hadn't noticed her before. She must have come in after the ceremony began.

When Rinaldo nudged her again, more urgently this time, Jillian murmured her answer, almost inaudibly. What else could she do? There was no escape. The priest was concluding the ceremony.

"Does anyone know why this man and this woman should not be joined in holy matrimony?"

It was only a formality, so they were all startled when the woman with the baby stood up and declared in a ringing voice, "I can give you a very good reason. Rinaldo has already made a commitment. He promised to marry *me!* This is his baby." She held up the infant wrapped in a pink blanket. As her words reverberated off the ancient walls, the baby in her arms began to cry.

After an instant of shocked silence, everybody started to talk at once: the woman, Rinaldo, the priest and the few spectators. Everybody but Jillian. She stared speechlessly at Rinaldo as he tried to fend off accusations from every side.

Finally he became aware of her stunned silence. Taking both of her hands, he held them tightly. "I am so sorry Maria had to spoil our beautiful wedding."

"You know her? That means she isn't some kind of deranged person who just wandered in by accident. Is she telling the truth? Are you the father of her baby?''

"Well, uh, it's a little complicated. But trust me, *cara*. If you'll just be patient, I'm sure everything will still work out.''

Jillian stared at him incredulously. "You can't really believe that!''

"We have to talk, darling. But not here. We'll go someplace quieter.''

Everybody was converging on them. Maria was shouting at him over the baby's wails, the priest was trying to question both of them, and the parishioners were crowding around so they wouldn't miss anything.

Jillian yanked her hands away from Rinaldo's grip and ran down the aisle to the door.

Once outside the church, she kept running through the winding cobblestone streets until she came to a quiet neighborhood of elegant villas along the Grand Canal. When she was too breathless to go any further, she sat on the sea wall between two palazzos, staring out at the activity on the water without really seeing it. She was numb with disbelief that something like this had really happened. The ugly scene in the church played over and over in her mind like a bad dream that wouldn't end.

When she was a little calmer, Jillian wondered what to do next. Her money was almost gone, but returning home wasn't an option. How could she face all the friends and family who had urged her not to rush into marriage? She would never hear the end of it! Yet what other choice did she have?

Sunk in misery and searching for a solution, she didn't see a speedboat rounding the bend at a terrific clip, sending up a sheet of water that soaked her from head to toe.

The man driving the boat looked like a gondolier in his white open-neck shirt and a scarf tied around his throat. The late afternoon sun turned his thick, dark hair to sable and outlined classic Roman features in a deeply tanned face. He was stunningly handsome, although Jillian was too upset at this latest indignity to notice.

He tied up to a pier in front of the impressive Venetian villa on her right and leapt out onto the sea wall, seemingly in one lithe movement. Extending a hand to help her up, he said in Italian, "I'm terribly sorry. I hope I haven't ruined your dress."

"That's the least of my worries," she muttered in his language, pushing the wet hair off her face. "I didn't intend to wear it again."

His interest quickened as he took a closer look at her. Were those orange blossoms in her hair? And that filmy white dress with a design of pearls around the neckline could easily be an afternoon wedding gown. But what was she doing here all alone? Surely no man would leave such a gorgeous woman waiting at the altar. If that wasn't what happened, why was she sitting here by herself looking so dejected?

"You must be very uncomfortable in those wet clothes. Come inside and let me give you some towels to dry yourself. My name is Gianni and I live here.'' He indicated the villa overlooking the dock he'd used.

It was an offer she could scarcely refuse. The alternative would be to walk back to the hotel with dripping hair and her gown plastered to her body like a wet rag. Everyone she passed would stare and snicker.

The splendor of the villa momentarily distracted her. Thick rugs covered the marble floors, and damask draperies were looped back from tall windows that gave a stunning view of the canal in front and gardens on the side. The furniture looked to be of museum quality, like the paintings in carved gilt frames and the exquisite ornaments scattered on shelves and tables.

''Come with me and I'll find something for you to wear while your clothes are being dried and pressed.'' Gianni stood at the foot of the curving staircase, waiting for Jillian to follow him.

She hesitated for just a moment before deciding she had nothing to worry about. This man was obviously someone of importance. He was also gorgeous, she noted belatedly. He didn't have to make a pass at any female, especially one who looked like a half-drowned cat.

She followed him up the stairs and into a baronial bedroom—a suite actually. While he went through another door, into a dressing room perhaps, she gazed around the luxurious suite.

A king-size bed sat royally on a low platform. The

bed was covered by a dark blue velvet spread with a geometric pattern embroidered in gold thread. Draperies at the tall windows were made of the same fabric.

At the opposite end of the room was a sitting area. A sofa and two large, comfortable-looking chairs were grouped around a marble-faced fireplace. A long table in front of it held books and magazines. Several photographs in silver frames were scattered around on end tables, but Gianni returned before Jillian could examine them.

He was carrying a white silk Japanese-style robe with wide sleeves. "You can put this on while your clothes are being attended to. Just leave them on the bed. I'll send a servant for them."

"Thank you. You're being very thoughtful."

"It's the least I can do after soaking you to the skin. You'll find a hair dryer in the bathroom, if you care to use it. Come downstairs for coffee when you're ready. I'll be in the den. It's the room to the right of the entry."

After he left, Jillian went into the bathroom to change. It was as magnificent as the rest of the suite, and very masculine. The walls, floor and countertops were brown marble flecked with white, and one complete wall was mirrored.

She took a dismayed look at her hair. She was still wearing the circlet of orange blossoms that almost screeched, "bride." What must Gianni think? Maybe he'd be too polite to ask questions. She threw the circlet in the wastebasket and reached for the hair dryer built into the wall.

When Jillian went downstairs a short time later, Gianni was working at a large, antique desk in the den, a comfortably furnished room with leather bound books lining two walls from floor to ceiling. Even in casual clothes, he looked as if he belonged in these luxurious surroundings.

Jillian wished she could feel the same. She was very uncomfortable wearing a thin robe with only a brief pair of lace panties underneath, considering the circumstances. Gianni was a total stranger, and a very virile one at that. She glanced down to make sure the robe was fastened securely.

A flash of desire lit Gianni's eyes as he gazed at her. He'd been too preoccupied before to realize how exquisite she was. With that lovely auburn hair floating free and natural around her shoulders, and the soft fabric of his dressing gown hinting at the curved body underneath, she looked as if she'd just gotten out of bed after making love. His loins tightened as he imagined what a night of passion with her would be like.

When Jillian glanced up, Gianni's expression was pleasant, nothing more. "Did you find everything you needed, *signorina…?*" he paused, looking at her expectantly.

She realized he wanted to know her name so she told him, then said, "Yes, thank you. I put the towels in the hamper, and I left my dress in the bathroom because it was so wet. If somebody could just

put it in the dryer for a few minutes that will be fine.
I don't care what it looks like.''

"I'm sure we can do better than that for you. I'd
feel badly if it were ruined. It's a lovely gown.''

"I thought so when I bought it, but I've changed
my mind.''

Rinaldo had gone shopping with her. In fact, he
was the one who picked it out. A friend of his owned
the dress shop, and they'd both urged her to buy the
dress, even though it was a lot more than she wanted
to spend. Had Rinaldo gotten a commission, Jillian
wondered now? The thought would never have occurred to her before today, but her trust in him had
clearly been misplaced. Nothing about Rinaldo
would surprise her now.

"Come sit on the couch,'' Gianni said.

As he came over to take the chair next to it there
was a light tap at the door. A dignified butler in a
black suit entered, carrying a baroque tray that held
a sterling silver coffee service. While the man set
the tray on the table in front of them and poured
coffee into two delicate bone china cups, Gianni told
him where to find Jillian's sodden dress.

When the man had left the room, she said, "You
have a beautiful home. I've seen these big palazzos
from water taxis. I always wondered if people really
lived in them as I was told.''

"Now you know it's true.'' He smiled. "You
don't live here in Venice?''

"No, I'm just visiting. I'm sure you can tell by
my accent that I'm not Italian.''

"You have a slight foreign accent that's barely noticeable. You speak our language like a native. What country are you from?"

"The United States. It's nice to hear that my accent is acceptable. I was a language major in college. After graduation I took a job in a private school teaching Italian and French."

"So you visit the two countries periodically to hone your skills?"

"I told myself this could be considered a business trip." Jillian smiled for the first time, remembering how she'd rationalized the expense. "Actually this is my first visit to Venice."

"I hope it won't be your last."

Her smile faded. "I doubt if I'll ever come back."

"I'd be very sorry to think that my carelessness was responsible for your decision."

"You weren't to blame. I should have picked someplace else to sit, but your wall was handy—although not a very prudent choice." She tried to make a joke of the incident. "But it's no big deal. All the travel articles say you should be prepared for little mishaps."

"That's a very healthy attitude. Perhaps you'll reconsider and give Venice another chance after all."

"I doubt that very much." When she realized her statement sounded impolite, Jillian said, "Venice is a magical city, but there are so many other places I haven't been."

"Is this just a brief stop on your grand tour?"

"No, that didn't work out. My sister and I had

intended to tour Europe together after she graduated from college, but her plans changed.''

''That's too bad. I hope it wasn't because of anything serious.''

''You might call it that.'' Jillian smiled. ''Bettina decided she'd rather get married.''

''That *is* serious,'' Gianni remarked in a sardonic tone. ''Did she opt for one of those big weddings with all the hoopla?''

''There were a lot of showers and parties ahead of time, but the wedding itself was a simple ceremony in the garden of our parents' home. Bettina and her fiancé, David, decided they could make better use of the money a lavish wedding would cost. They're both only twenty-one and planning to go to graduate school.''

''They sound very sensible.''

''Yes, it was a surprise to all of us. I was always considered the levelheaded one, and Bettina was the impulsive teenager.'' Jillian's mouth twisted in a self-mocking grimace.

Gianni gazed at her covertly, wondering what had gone wrong with her life. She seemed especially blessed by nature. ''I'm sure it was a lovely wedding,'' he commented. ''Were you the maid…or perhaps the matron of honor?''

''Maid of honor—I'm not married.''

She'd heard about *that* over and over again! Her friends had asked, ''What's wrong with you? Tom—'' or Evan or Charlie or whoever she was going with at the time ''—is a great catch and he's crazy about you.''

Her mother had been even more blunt. ''It's time you settled down and started a family. What are you waiting for? Your dream man? Only teenagers believe they'll meet him in real life.''

Jillian had given a joking response to all of them, but she secretly worried that perhaps she *was* looking for someone who didn't exist.

''I suppose you needed a vacation after all the activity of the wedding,'' Gianni prompted, after she remained silent for long moments. Nothing she'd told him explained the orange blossoms in her hair, or what she'd been doing on his sea wall, all alone and sad. ''Is that why you came to Venice?''

''Even the best of weddings are stressful,'' she answered evasively. Why was he asking all these questions? His interest in her, a total stranger, seemed suspect. Jillian no longer trusted any man's intentions. She decided to ask her own questions. ''You sound as if you know a lot about weddings. Did you have one of those large, formal affairs?''

''No. Like you, I'm unmarried.''

''You live in this big house all alone?''

''Except for the servants.'' He nodded.

''I can't imagine living alone in a place this huge.''

''The solitude seems like a blessing after my nephews leave.'' He chuckled. ''I'm very fond of them, but nine-year-old twin boys prove there *is* such a thing as perpetual motion.''

"Do you have a lot of nieces and nephews?"

"No, Angelina is my only sibling, and I doubt if she'll have more children. Joseph and Roberto seem to have satisfied her maternal instinct."

"Well, at least you have the two boys. I'm looking forward to being an aunt, but I'm afraid it's going to be a long wait. Bettina and David have years of schooling ahead of them."

"I'm sure you're happy for your sister, but it's too bad she couldn't make this trip with you."

Jillian's face sobered. "Yes, it could have been so great."

"You'll forget any unpleasantness once you're back home with your family," Gianni said gently. "We tend to remember only the good parts of a vacation as time passes."

For a short while she'd managed to put aside the trauma she'd been through, and the dilemma she still faced. Now her problems resurfaced. This man was undoubtedly someone important, and he'd been very kind. Maybe he could help her.

"I'm sure you're right about remembering only the good things, but I didn't have any really bad experiences here," she said in a carefully casual voice. "As a matter of fact, I'd like to stay for a few more weeks. I mean, Venice is a long way from California. I might as well see everything while I'm here."

"That sounds sensible."

"The only problem is, I'd have to get a job in order to stay on. Would you happen to know of anybody who is looking for temporary help? Maybe in an office as a replacement worker while the regular employees take their vacations. I'm very good at computers. Or I could be a tutor, or a cashier in a restaurant. I'd be willing to do almost anything legitimate.'' Jillian hated the pleading note in her voice, but she didn't know where else to turn.

She looked so young and vulnerable that Gianni wanted to take her in his arms and tell her not to worry, that he'd make all her troubles go away. Unfortunately she was asking for something that, even with his connections, couldn't be done—at least not immediately, as she was hoping.

''I'd work for the absolute minimum wage,'' she said when he hesitated. ''I just need enough to pay for my hotel room. The Monaco is a little tourist place that caters to people on a budget. They might even give me a lower rate if I stay for an extended period.''

''If that's your only problem, I'll be able to help you there. You can be my houseguest for a couple of weeks.''

''I wasn't angling for an invitation,'' she protested.

''I didn't think you were. But it's an easy solution. As you can see, I have plenty of room.''

''You're very kind, but I couldn't possibly accept,'' she said firmly. ''I *would* accept your help in getting a job, though.''

''I wish you had asked for something simpler. It's very difficult for a foreigner to work in Venice,'' he explained. "You would need a work permit, which could take months—and that's assuming you could even get one. They issue them very sparingly."

"I'm not surprised. I think it's the same in the U.S."

"I might be able to cut through some of the red tape, but you'd still have to be prepared to wait for weeks."

"That's the trouble. I can't wait." Her slender shoulders slumped. "Well, thanks anyway. Maybe I'll just have to bite the bullet and go home."

"How long can you hang on? Perhaps something will occur to me."

Before Jillian could answer, the butler entered after a discreet knock. "Scusami, signore, but the Countess of Rivoli wishes to speak to you on the telephone," he announced.

"Tell her I'm engaged at the moment," Gianni said. "I'll have to call her back."

As the man turned to leave, Jillian said, "You can take your call. My dress must be dry by now. I'll go upstairs and change."

The butler had paused, but Gianni waved him out, saying to Jillian, "You don't need to rush off. I'll order some fresh coffee. Or perhaps you'd like something stronger?"

She shook her head. "I've taken up enough of your time." She was embarrassed at having asked him for a favor—and then being turned down. He must think she was a real opportunist!

Jillian rose from the couch, but in her hurry to

get away she stumbled on the long trailing robe. It flew open, and as if that wasn't bad enough, she pitched forward, right into Gianni's arms!

He had risen when she did, and he caught her automatically—even in his bemused state. The unexpected sight of her slim, almost nude body confirmed what he already suspected. Beneath that innocent, angelic face was the flawless body of a siren! His hands moved unconsciously over her smooth skin.

Jillian's cheeks bloomed like wild roses as she tried to untangle her feet and regain her balance. Could anything more happen to her on this wretched day? She was relieved when she could stand on her own and Gianni released her.

"I seem to be especially accident prone today," she said, trying for a light tone, but unable to look at him.

"Neither incident was your fault." He tried mightily not to laugh as she pulled her belt so tight he was afraid she'd cut off her circulation.

"Yes, well, I'd better get out of here before anything else happens." Without waiting for an answer, she hiked the robe up to her knees and almost ran to the door.

Gianni didn't try to stop her, knowing how embarrassed she was. It had actually bothered her that he'd caught a glimpse of her lovely body. He could have told her that a lot of women would kill for a figure like hers, but she wouldn't have considered it a compliment. Jillian wasn't like the sophisticated women he knew.

She wasn't like any woman he'd ever known. Her charming air of innocence was very refreshing. Unfortunately some unprincipled swine had taken advantage of it. He wondered what had happened, then decided he didn't want to know. He would rather remember her incredibly blue eyes, and the enchanting way she'd smiled, those few times she'd forgotten her troubles temporarily.

Jillian didn't want to remember Gianni. She longed to forget everything that had happened this dreadful day!

She dressed hastily, noticing without interest that his servants had done a superb job of restoring her gown. It looked brand-new. Not that she'd ever consider wearing it again, but at least she wouldn't have to slink back to the hotel.

Jillian would have preferred to slip out of the house without having to face Gianni again, but she couldn't very well leave without thanking him for his hospitality. Her innate good manners wouldn't permit it, even though she'd never see him again.

For once, luck was with her. She heard his voice as she approached the den. Gianni must have returned his earlier phone call. While she hesitated in the hallway, the butler appeared.

"I'm leaving now," she told the man. "Please give the signore my thanks and tell him I didn't want to disturb him."

As she walked rapidly away from the villa, Jillian realized that she'd never found out Gianni's last name. Had he assumed that she knew who he was? Anyone that rich and self-assured was probably well-known. He was handsome and virile enough to be an Italian movie star. She'd discovered just *how* virile when her bare breasts had been crushed against his hard chest.

During those embarrassing few moments while she struggled to regain her balance, she'd become intimately acquainted with the rest of his impressive physique. If Rinaldo hadn't soured her on the entire male gender—at least for the foreseeable future—she could have been attracted to Gianni. Tall, lean men with compelling charm had always appealed to her. No more, though!

The only thing that interested her now was how she could manage to remain in Venice with no job and rapidly dwindling finances. Jillian lifted her chin, refusing to accept defeat. Something would turn up. If she'd lived through this ghastly day she could survive anything!

Chapter Two

Gianni was disappointed to find out Jillian had left.
He wished he could have gotten to know her better.
But he knew she wouldn't have been receptive.
Whatever had happened to her here in Venice had
made her wary of all men. If he'd asked to see her
again, even for something as unthreatening as lunch,
she would almost certainly have refused.

Since it was unlikely that they would ever meet
again, Gianni expected to forget all about Jillian. He
was surprised to find himself thinking about her off
and on all that evening, and even the next morning.
It was probably the air of mystery that surrounded
her, he decided. A mystery that was especially intriguing because it would remain unsolved.

A telephone call from his secretary later in the morning seemed like some kind of omen, more than just a coincidence. Bella was a competent woman in her late thirties, who had worked for Gianni for quite a while. She'd almost given up hope of having a baby, so she and her husband were ecstatic when she finally got pregnant after trying unsuccessfully for years. But now in her eighth month complications had developed.

"The doctor warned me that it wouldn't be as easy at my age," she sighed. "He wants me to stay in bed for at least a couple of weeks, maybe longer."

"Then that's exactly what you should do," Gianni told her.

"But you're giving that huge costume ball in a month. How will you manage without me?"

"Don't even think about it. Your job right now is to take care of yourself so I can be a godfather."

"I know you're right, but I just hate leaving you in the lurch. There are so many things to do. Men don't realize that. Do you think you can get somebody to take over for me temporarily?"

"As a matter of fact, I just met a young woman who is looking for work. I'll give her a call."

"I didn't realize I could be replaced so easily," she said in a miffed tone. "I guess I needn't have worried."

Gianni hid his amusement as he hastened to reassure her. "I'll be completely lost without you. This person could never take your place, but at least she'll be here to answer the phone and check off the acceptances and refusals.''

"There's a lot more to do than that." Bella proceeded to give him a long list of instructions to pass along. She finally concluded by saying, "I'm sure it will be confusing. Tell her to call me if she has any problems."

After cradling the receiver, Gianni tried to remember the name of Jillian's hotel. Something with an *M*. Moroni? Moresco? No, Monaco!

Jillian's gloom turned to incredulous joy when she heard Gianni's offer. "Of course I'm interested! I don't care if it's only for a couple of weeks. I'd love to have the job."

"Splendid. When can you start? Bella has only been gone for two days and things are already starting to pile up."

"I can come over right now."

By the time Jillian arrived, Gianni was starting to have a few reservations. It was a nice feeling to be able to help someone, and he would enjoy having her around. It was the chance he wanted, to get to know her better.

But he really did need a secretary. Was Jillian a wise choice? Why was she so determined to stay in Venice after she'd had a bad experience here? Would she change her mind after a few days and decide to go home? Perhaps he'd be better off with temporary help from an agency. Anyone they sent would be guaranteed to stay until Bella returned to work.

Jillian wasn't aware of any of these negative thoughts as she sat across the desk from Gianni in Bella's office. Her face was lit up like a sunrise.

He groaned inwardly. She looked so young and eager. How could he withdraw his offer? It would be like kicking a kitten. But at least he had to find out something about her.

"I really think we should talk it over before you commit yourself to taking this job," he began.

He couldn't be having second thoughts! Jillian rushed to present her credentials. "I know I can handle it. I'm familiar with all kinds of computers, and I can write business letters and file. I can even do some light bookkeeping if that's what you need."

"I'm sure you're very competent, but I also require someone I can count on. I'm having a large party that will require a lot of coordination on your part. It would be very inconvenient for me if you suddenly became homesick, and I had to bring in somebody else."

Returning home to face all the embarrassing questions that would be asked was the last thing Jillian wanted to do. But Gianni couldn't be expected to take her word for it. She'd have to tell him at least part of the story.

"I understand your concern, but you needn't worry," she said. "I have a good reason for not wanting to go home. I told everybody I was getting married, and then…my plans changed. It would be a little awkward to explain what happened.''

So he was right about her being jilted, Gianni thought. ''I'm sorry you were disappointed. Unfortunately a lot of men make promises they don't intend to keep,'' he said gently.

''I wish Rinaldo hadn't kept the one he made to me!'' she blurted out before she could stop herself.

Gianni gave her a puzzled frown. ''I don't understand. When I found you alone on my doorstep, dressed for a wedding with orange blossoms in your hair, I assumed the groom had left you waiting at the church.''

''No, he showed up—and so did the mother of his child. Rinaldo had promised to marry her, too, but he never got around to it.'' Jillian realized that Gianni wouldn't be satisfied with a few sketchy details. She'd have to tell him everything.

''How long had you known this man?''

''Not long enough, obviously.'' She had picked up the disapproval he couldn't quite hide. This was just a small sample of what she faced at home. ''I'm usually very levelheaded, but there's something about the romance of Venice.''

''And you were probably lonely.'' He nodded.

''I thought I might be when I decided to come without Bettina, but I really wasn't. Everybody was so friendly.''

Gianni wasn't surprised. He could imagine how many men had tried to pick her up.

''I spent my days wandering around Venice, and

at night I sometimes dropped into a little club to listen to some music and have a cappuccino. That's where I met Rinaldo. He was very handsome and very smooth.'' She paused remembering how Rinaldo had come on to her. And how surprised he'd been when she was merely amused.

Gianni reached a different conclusion. "He swept you off your feet?"

"Well, let's just say he tried. But I'm not that naive. I thanked him for the cappuccino and told him I'd enjoyed talking to him, and then I got up to leave. But Rinaldo was clever. He realized that he'd come on too strong and I would refuse to go out on a regular date with him, so he asked me to go for a vaporetto ride around Venice the next day."

Gianni was looking at her with a raised eyebrow. "That was scarcely an inducement. You must have been on a vaporetto during your stay here. Those water buses are the main means of public transportation in Venice."

"Yes, but I didn't know what I was looking at. We'd pass these fascinating ancient buildings and I didn't know what they were. Rinaldo said he'd be my private tour guide. I couldn't see anything wrong with that. We'd be surrounded by people in broad daylight."

"However, it didn't stop there?"

"No, but Rinaldo was a perfect gentleman, and it was nice to have a companion to share all the beautiful sights with. When he asked me to have dinner with him, I accepted."

"And that's when he stopped being a perfect gentleman," Gianni commented dryly.

"Not right away. He took me to a little trattoria with lots of atmosphere and we talked all through dinner. I realize now that he didn't tell me anything about himself. He asked all about *my* life, even where I went to college. I told him I'd graduated from the University of California Los Angeles and had gone back to live in my home town of Sacramento. I was surprised that he'd heard of it because it isn't that well-known in foreign countries, although it's the capital of California.

"Rinaldo wanted to know all about my family, so I told him my father owns a department store in downtown Sacramento, and my mother helps out occasionally at holiday times. Usually, though, she's busy with her various charity organizations."

"All of his questions didn't make you suspicious?" Gianni asked.

"Not really. I guess like most people, I was flattered to have somebody so interested in me. To give the devil his due, Rinaldo is a very attractive man."

Gianni's distaste was reflected in his voice when he said, "I suppose he suggested going back to his apartment after dinner."

"Yes, but I refused, and he didn't seem annoyed. We took a walk around the back streets of Venice instead, and then sat on a bench in one of those charming little squares. That's when he made his move."

Gianni could imagine the scene. The cobblestone

streets were dimly lit at night, away from the tourist haunts. What he couldn't understand was why she hadn't ended the relationship right then!

She could tell from Gianni's expression what he was thinking. "I was very angry because he pretended he'd gotten my message—that I wasn't interested. I told Rinaldo I never wanted to see him again, and I left him there in the square.

"The next day he sent me a huge bouquet of roses. He'd found out at dinner the night before where I was staying. I hung up on him when he followed the flowers with a phone call, but he was waiting for me in front of my hotel when I went out. He was so apologetic and so…well, sort of boyishly penitent, that I couldn't stay angry at him. After all, he didn't try to force himself on me."

"So you agreed to go on seeing him."

"It seemed easier than having him follow me around like a spaniel with mournful eyes." She sighed. "I wish I could tell you how things got so out of hand, but I don't understand it myself. Rinaldo never tried to make love to me again, but he was…very romantic." Jillian's cheeks were pink as she glanced down at her tightly clasped hands.

Again, Gianni got the picture. This Rinaldo's experience was far greater than hers. She'd never known a man completely without scruples, so she had no defense against him. He turned up the heat gradually until she was excited and confused.

"When Rinaldo asked me to marry him I told him it was too soon, that we didn't know each other well enough.'' Jillian was in a hurry now to finish her embarrassing story. ''He convinced me that if two people were in love it was foolish to wait. When I was alone, I wasn't even sure I loved him, but I was seldom alone. And as soon as we were together the next day, my doubts seemed foolish. I did insist on telling my parents, but when they told me all the things I'd told Rinaldo, I got defensive.

''After that, everything speeded up. He picked the church and took me to buy my wedding gown. Before I knew it I was standing at the altar. I wish I'd slept with him like he wanted!'' she burst out. ''At least I'd have been spared that terrible scene at the church.''

''I'm sure he would have been delighted to make love to you, but it wouldn't have changed the outcome,'' Gianni said. ''His ultimate goal was to marry you. Men like Rinaldo are predators. They see female tourists, especially American ones, as meal tickets.''

''But I'm not rich! I'm staying at a modest hotel, and I have to watch every penny.''

''You told him your father owns a department store.''

''A small one founded by my grandfather. Colby's has been in business for a long time, but my father was never interested in expanding it or opening other stores. He was content to make a comfortable living and spend time with his family.''

''Rinaldo might have had his own agenda. Perhaps he planned to ease your father out and take over once you were married.''

"Rinaldo has the morals of an alley cat, but I can scarcely believe he'd marry me to get his hands on my father's money," she protested. "Even *he* couldn't be that underhanded."

"I could be wrong." Gianni didn't press the point.

It was a new and disturbing idea. If Gianni was right, then her judgment had been even worse than she thought, Jillian reflected morosely. At the age of twenty-six, she should have been more astute. Gianni must think she was a real airhead! The problem now was convincing him that she was a mature woman, capable of handling his job.

She took a deep breath and said, "I probably told you more than you cared to hear. But I wanted you to know why this job means so much to me, why I won't suddenly decide to leave. It's my only chance to stay in Venice."

He stared at her with a slight frown. "After all that's happened, why would you want to stay?"

"I don't hold Venice responsible." Her attempt at a smile faded. "The real reason is that I raved on and on about Rinaldo and how happy we were together. How can I go home and tell everybody I changed my mind? I certainly can't admit the truth—that he's a con artist and worse. It would be too humiliating!"

"You'll have to tell them sooner or later."

"I know, but I thought I'd say we had an argu-

ment and called off the wedding. They can't expect
me to go into every little detail on the phone. Long-
distance rates are too expensive. I figure if I can
hang on till the end of summer, the whole thing will
have blown over. By the time I do go home they'll
be used to the idea and we'll have other things to
talk about.''

"Won't your family wonder why you don't come
home as you'd planned, as long as the wedding is
off?''

"That's another reason I was so desperate to get
a job. It gives me a believable reason for staying
longer.''

"You seem to have thought this out thoroughly,
but wouldn't it make you sound less impulsive if
you said that you and Rinaldo decided to postpone
the wedding until you got to know each other better.
That seems like a more credible reason for wanting
to stay here.''

"What a good idea! I can ease out of the situation
by telling them we're still engaged. Then I can say
we decided we're not right for each other. After all,
Rinaldo and I spent a relatively short time together,
and a broken engagement isn't as serious as a can-
celed wedding. Actually my parents will be relieved.''

"So you're just doing this for them,'' Gianni
teased.

"Don't nominate me for sainthood quite yet.''
She laughed, then her face sobered. "I really am
trying to make it easier for all of us. They'd be very

concerned about me if they knew the truth. But no lasting damage was done. I realize now that I wasn't really in love with Rinaldo. And hopefully I learned something from the experience."

"I don't believe you ever mentioned his last name," Gianni said in a casual tone.

"Rinaldo Marsala," she said with distaste. Jillian didn't want to discuss him anymore. "If I've convinced you that I'll stay as long as you need me, perhaps you can tell me what I'm supposed to do."

"You'll be in charge of details for a party I'm giving next month. It's going to be a masked ball for five hundred or so people, and as you can imagine, it entails a lot of preparation. Bella has already hired the caterer, the florist and the other necessary people. All the preliminary work is done, but you'll have to confer with them and coordinate everything."

Jillian's eyes widened as she realized for the first time who this man was whom she'd been talking to so freely. When he mentioned a masked ball the pieces clicked into place. He was Gianni di Destino, the Duke of Venezia. One of the richest, most sought after bachelors in Italy, if not the entire continent!

The local newspapers had been buzzing for days about the costume ball he was giving. Merchants, hotel keepers and restauranteurs were rubbing their hands together in anticipation. Gianni's guests—a mixture of royalty, socialites, celebrities and the just plain wealthy—were flying in from all over the world with plenty of money to spend.

And she would be in the middle of it! Jillian gazed at him with shining eyes as she tried to concentrate on what he was saying.

"You don't need any special expertise for the job, but it will be very time-consuming. Especially as the date approaches."

"I won't mind working long hours. I don't have anything else to do."

"Just so you understand there is a lot involved. Also, some of the people you'll be working with can be very temperamental." He gazed at her lovely, ingenuous face with a hint of misgiving. "Do you think you can handle them?"

"After dealing with prima donnas on the faculty, and demanding parents who think their child should receive all of your attention, this will be a piece of cake."

"As long as you know what you're getting into. Of course you'll have as much help as you need, and if you have any serious problems you can always come to me."

"I'm sure that won't be necessary. I intend to do such a good job that you won't even know I'm here."

"I doubt if that's true."

Something flickered in his tawny eyes as he gazed at her. But his expression changed so swiftly that Jillian wondered if she'd imagined the subtly male look on his face. She must have. Gianni could have his pick of titled, glamorous women on several continents. Why would he give a second thought to someone ordinary like herself?

He was glancing at his watch. "I'm sorry to have to leave you on your first day, but I have to go out. Suppose you start by opening the accumulation of mail. There will be a lot of RSVPs. Bella has a guest list around here someplace, probably in the file cabinet. When you find it, check off the acceptances and refusals."

Jillian nodded without comment, although she couldn't believe that anyone would turn down an invitation to what would surely be the most talked about party of the year.

They discussed other things she could do in his absence, and then Gianni left her alone.

He didn't leave the house immediately. First he went into the den and closed the door while he made a phone call to his attorney.

"I want you to hire a detective agency to check out a small-time lothario named Rinaldo Marsala," Gianni said. "He hangs around the tourist haunts, picking up gullible females."

"Do you suspect him of a sex crime?" Enrico, the other man, asked. "If so, it's a matter for the police."

"He's a con man, not a thug. Venice would be better off without his kind, but they're like cockroaches. I don't suppose we'll ever get rid of them completely."

"But you want him investigated." The attorney

was clearly curious, yet he knew better than to ask questions. Gianni was a very private person.

"Yes, do a thorough job. Just don't use my name. And I'd like the results as soon as possible."

Gianni realized that some people might think he was going to a lot of trouble for a woman he barely knew. But it was clearly the humanitarian thing to do. The fact that Jillian was young and strikingly beautiful had nothing to do with it. Well, very little anyway, he grinned.

Chapter Three

Jillian couldn't wait to get to work the next morning. She and Gianni hadn't discussed what her hours would be, but she was up and out of the hotel early.

To her surprise, Gianni had been up even earlier. Marco, the butler, told her that Gianni was already gone. Jillian had just assumed that he slept till noon after partying all night. Wasn't that the lifestyle of the rich and famous? Was this just one of her many misconceptions about him?

"The duke left instructions for you on your desk," Marco said. He was a tall, imposing man with an expressionless face. He led her down the hall and left her at the door.

Bella's office was bright and cheerful, with the

sun streaming in and a view of the side garden through the windows that lined one wall. The furnishings were modern and functional, as opposed to the priceless antiques in the rest of the palazzo. In addition to the large desk, there were several file cabinets, a couple of chairs and a small couch covered in a colorful print.

The note from Gianni was very businesslike. He briefly but concisely outlined the things that needed to be done. Jillian couldn't help being a little disappointed by his terseness. After his warmth and understanding the day before, she thought they'd become friends. Well, maybe not friends, but they'd established a sort of rapport. Evidently that was only her interpretation. She was just an employee here—which was the way she wanted it. The duke lived in a faster-paced world than hers.

Jillian was hard at work when Gianni returned around noon. He was dressed casually in fawn colored slacks and a silk knit polo shirt.

"Did you find everything all right?" he asked. "I'm sorry I wasn't here to help you get started, but I had a long-standing date to play golf."

"I didn't know people played golf here," she said.

"Did you think Italians only lived to eat, drink and make love to pretty girls?" he teased.

"Well, not necessarily in that order," she answered, her eyes sparkling mischievously.

"I can see I'll have to change your opinion of Italian men."

"You already have," she answered. That was true, but Jillian didn't want him to take it personally. "What I meant was, where did they find enough land in Venice to build a golf course?"

"It's just across the canal on Lido Isle. You must have been there to the casino, or the Hotel des Bains."

"Very briefly."

Rinaldo had taken her to the Lido on a vaporetto, and they'd gone inside the gambling casino just for a quick look. She had wanted to stay longer at the wonderful old hotel, and had suggested having an espresso on the terrace facing the large, raised swimming pool. Rinaldo told her they'd do it the next time. He said he'd forgotten to go to the bank and was short on cash. She had heard the hotel was very pricey, but even dazzled by infatuation, she'd wondered if he wasn't a tiny bit cheap. Two little cups of coffee couldn't be that expensive.

"The Lido deserves more than a brief look," Gianni said. "Perhaps we can have lunch there one day and drive around the island."

"That would be nice," Jillian answered politely, suspecting it was one of those vague invitations that would never materialize. "I opened the mail and made a separate pile of things that need your attention. Mostly it was party related. There were dozens of acceptances to the ball."

"How many can't make it?"

"Only two. Baron Stanhope is in the hospital preparing for open heart surgery, and Lily Marchand's daughter is getting married that night. Her note said she was devastated that she couldn't attend the ball, but her daughter would never speak to her again if she skipped her wedding.''

Gianni chuckled. ''Lily hates to miss a party.''

''Especially this one. It's going to be fantastic!'' Jillian had looked over the menu, the florist's sketches and the multitude of other preparations.

''I think it will be amusing. No one has given a costume ball in a while and people like to pretend to be someone else. They can do all sorts of naughty things when their identities are hidden behind a mask.''

''It's the kind of thing the tabloids love, too,'' Jillian commented. ''They'll probably all send photographers.''

''I've arranged for security, but I'm sure they'll get some pictures anyway. My guests are used to it, and there is nothing new they can say about me. My life is an open book by now.''

Duke di Destino wasn't as well known in America, but Jillian knew a little about him from the Venetian newspapers. He was thirty-four, had never been married, and was heir to a vast fortune. The House of Destino had a noble lineage going back hundreds of years.

''If you don't have any questions, I'd like to take a quick shower before lunch,'' he said.

''I did want to talk to you about one thing. I noticed you have a computer over on that table by the window, but your secretary hasn't been using it.''

Gianni smiled. "Bella is remarkably set in her ways for a young woman. But you have to understand. Computers aren't as omnipresent here as they are in your country. She had a few mishaps while she was trying to learn, and after that she flatly refused to use 'that machine from hell' as she put it."

"I know it can be confusing at first, but a computer can greatly simplify things—like your guest list. She has the names written on sheets of paper, not in very clear order. Sometimes she just penciled in additions at the end of a page. I had to go through the whole list to check off the newest responses. It would save a lot of time if everything was in alphabetical order on the computer. I could scroll through the names in a fraction of the time."

"Then feel free to do it that way. I'll see you later."

It took time to transfer Bella's lists. Some names were duplicated and others had little notations after them that were difficult to read. Jillian was hard at work when Gianni reappeared.

"Have you had lunch already?" he asked.

"No, I'm still transferring data to the computer." She glanced at her watch. "I didn't realize it had gotten so late."

"If you're trying to impress me with your diligence you've succeeded," he teased. "Now it's time to take a break."

She stood and arched her tired back. "I believe I will go out for a sandwich. I only had coffee this morning."

"Then a sandwich is not enough." Gianni glanced appreciatively at her slender figure. She had on a pale yellow knit pullover that outlined her high, firm breasts and narrow rib cage. "Come and join me for something more substantial."

"Maybe it *would* be faster."

"I hoped you would accept because you found me irresistible."

Jillian glanced at him warily and was reassured by the sparkle of merriment in his amber eyes. "I can't imagine any woman being able to resist you," she said lightly.

"That's what I was hoping to hear. I'll tell Marco to set another place. Meet me in the dining room in ten minutes."

The large dining room was quite formal. A polished mahogany table dominated the room, along with the massive crystal chandelier that hung over it. Twelve dining chairs upholstered in maroon satin with a design of gold fleurs-de-lis, were positioned around the table, which was centered by an exquisite Meissen urn filled with large, speckled lilies.

Jillian was a little daunted by such elegance. No wonder Gianni didn't want to eat in here alone! While she was gazing around, he appeared at the open French door leading to a walled garden.

"It's such a nice day that I thought you might enjoy having lunch outside," he said.

A round table was set with two gaily colored place mats that echoed the profusion of flowers blooming all around the patio in pots and in flower beds.

"This is so charming," Jillian remarked. "You don't expect to find a garden right in the middle of Venice."

"I only wish I had more time to enjoy it." Gianni seated her at the table, then took the wrought iron chair across from her.

"What else do you have to do?" she asked without thinking, then turned as pink as the camellias on a nearby bush. "I'm so sorry! That was very rude of me."

He looked amused. "You can't be blamed for thinking what so many others do, that I'm an indolent playboy who parties from dusk till dawn. My social life is written up extensively. I can't imagine why."

"It's fun to read about glamorous people living the kind of lives the rest of us can never hope to."

"I'm sure you lead a very interesting life at home." He looked at her softly curved mouth, envying all the men who were fortunate enough to have kissed her.

"You must know that ordinary people don't live like you do."

"If you're referring to yourself, I would never consider you ordinary." Gianni's voice was like velvet as he gazed at her.

Jillian knew the compliment wasn't meant to be taken seriously. Italian men were known for being charismatic and just naturally seductive, even when they didn't mean anything by it. Still, she felt more comfortable when a uniformed maid brought in their first course, slices of prosciutto and plump green figs served on exquisite china. Then Marco poured wine into their fluted glasses.

"This looks delicious, but I'd better skip the wine," Jillian said. "I have a lot of work to do this afternoon."

"You've been slaving away all morning. Perhaps I should get someone in to help you."

"No, I can handle it," she said swiftly. "I wasn't complaining. I love this job."

"Spending the morning putting names into a computer doesn't sound very interesting."

"That wasn't all I did. I talked to the most fascinating people! The Countess of Albion called to ask if she could bring another guest."

He looked at Jillian's animated face with amusement. "Ellie is a very nice person, but even her best friends wouldn't call her fascinating."

"She was very pleasant on the phone, even when I couldn't give her an answer. I told her I was new here, and I'd have to ask you if it would be all right. She said for you to call her."

"Do it for me. Tell her it's fine and add whoever it is to the list. I don't have time to sit on the phone with Ellie for an hour. I told my sister I would come by after lunch."

It was the first time he'd mentioned anything personal about himself. Jillian was curious to know more, but she didn't want to appear nosy. Keeping her voice casual, she remarked, "It's nice that you have a sister nearby."

Her ploy didn't work. Gianni changed the subject. "How did your family take the news that you postponed the wedding?"

"I didn't tell them yet."

He looked at her with a raised eyebrow. "You have to tell them. It will only get harder the longer you wait."

"I know," Jillian sighed. "But I'll have to answer at least some of their questions, and I'm not very good at lying."

"Just think of it as bending the truth a little. You did try to tell Rinaldo that it was too soon to rush into marriage, and you also told him you should get to know each other better first."

"That's true."

"So you won't be lying when you say the same things your parents told *you*."

"What if they don't believe I'd really want to stay if I had to get a job to do it? They might wonder if there is some other reason why I don't just come home."

"That wouldn't be logical if you're still engaged, which is the story you plan to tell. You and Rinaldo could scarcely get to know each other better if you were on different continents."

"Oh, that's right. I didn't think of that. You see? That's why I have trouble lying. There are too many details to keep track of."

"You'll get the hang of it." He grinned.

He sounded like a man with experience. How many women had believed him when he murmured words of love in their ear? Somebody like Gianni had an unfair advantage to begin with. He was handsome and charming, as well as extremely kind. She owed him a lot. But he was probably no different from any other man in his relationships with women. Could you trust any man? Jillian wondered somberly.

The maid wheeled in a lovely antique tea cart bearing a platter of steaming linguine that looked like an illustration in a gourmet magazine. Clams, mussels and huge rosy prawns almost covered the savory smelling pasta.

Jillian was momentarily distracted. "Good grief, this is considered an average lunch?"

"Italians believe in eating a proper meal. We'll never understand how you Americans can be satisfied with a hamburger, or that trifling little snack you call a B.L.T."

"How would you know what a bacon, lettuce and tomato sandwich is?" she exclaimed.

"From visits to your country. I was shocked to see what you people call lunch."

"I suppose you would be. Our main requirement is that it be fast and filling." She laughed. It was impossible to imagine Gianni in a fast-food place. "Where did you go in the U.S.?"

"I've been there often. I usually go to New York or Washington on business, but I did make one trip to California. I had promised my nephews a trip to

Los Angeles for their eighth birthday last year. They wanted to visit your movie studios and Disneyland.''

''You went to Disneyland?''

''Unfortunately, something came up unexpectedly and I couldn't go with them that day. Their nanny took them.''

Jillian wondered cynically if it had been a blonde or a brunette who ''came up unexpectedly.'' ''It isn't the kind of place that would interest you anyway,'' she said.

He looked at her with mild irritation. ''You think I manufactured an excuse to get out of going, but you're wrong. I enjoy being with my nephews. I like children.''

''They must be a lot of fun at that age,'' she said politely.

''Yes, but I enjoyed their toddler stage, too.''

''It's too bad you don't have some of your own. You certainly have enough room for a large family.''

''I said I like children. That doesn't mean I want a wife,'' he drawled.

''It's more convenient if it's a package deal,'' she commented dryly. ''Don't you ever expect to get married?''

''Possibly. But it isn't a priority. I don't believe people have to go through life two by two in order to be happy. That's a concept dreamed up by romantics.''

Jillian gazed down at her plate, realizing that

Gianni thought of her as one of those silly romantics. She'd certainly acted like one with Rinaldo.

"I wasn't referring to you." He reached across
the table and covered her hand with his. "You were
the victim of an unscrupulous con man."

That was true, but it didn't make her feel any
better. "At least I learned not to be so gullible. I
just hope my family never finds out."

"There's no reason why they should. Call them
right now. You'll feel better once it's off your
mind."

"I'll call them when I go back to the hotel after
work. It's apt to be a lengthy conversation, and I
don't want to put an expensive long-distance call on
your telephone."

"I'll take it out of your salary if that will make
you feel better. Do it now. Or at least, after you've
had dessert."

"I couldn't eat another thing," she assured him.
"This is more than I usually eat for dinner. In fact,
I'll probably skip dinner after this big meal."

"I can see your lifestyle needs changing. I'll have
to teach you the art of living well."

Jillian was sure he could teach her more than that,
but they were things she was better off not knowing.
Gianni and his friends lived in a different world
from her safe, normal one.

When she was back in her office a short time
later, Jillian reluctantly picked up the phone. She
knew Gianni wouldn't let up until she called her

parents, and it was the sensible thing to do. She couldn't postpone it for too much longer or she'd create more problems for herself.

They were delighted to hear from her. Before they could demand to hear every detail of the wedding, Jillian asked about her sister and assorted relatives.

Finally her mother said, "This phone call is costing you a fortune! Tell me quickly about the wedding, and then maybe we could say hello to our new son-in-law for a minute."

"Well, uh, I had a slight change of plans, Mom."

"What's wrong, dear?" Her mother was instantly concerned. "You sounded so happy the last time we talked to you. Did something happen?"

"Nothing bad. In fact, I think you'll be pleased." Jillian made an effort to sound upbeat. "You tried to talk me out of getting married. I know I wouldn't listen to you at the time, but I thought it over and I realized you were right."

"Oh, my dear, I'm so sorry! I shouldn't have interfered. Did you and your young man quarrel because of what I said?"

"No, we…he agreed with you." This was as difficult as Jillian feared it would be. "A whirlwind wedding would have been very romantic, but we decided we didn't know each other well enough to rush into marriage."

"I can't say I'm not relieved, but are you all right?"

"I'm fine, Mom. Don't worry about me."

"How can I help worrying? I think you made the

right decision, but you must be feeling let down. I
wish I could be there with you.''

"What's going on?'' a man's voice in the background demanded.

"They didn't get married,'' Sarah Colby told her
husband.

"Good! When is she coming home? Let me talk
to her.'' Ben Colby took the phone from his wife.
"How are you doing, honey?''

"Just great, Dad. I adore Venice. It's as fabulous
as I thought it would be.''

"But what's all this about you and your fiancé?
I can hardly believe you suddenly decided parents
know best,'' he said dryly.

"There's just no pleasing you, Dad,'' Jillian
teased.

His voice sobered. "What really happened to
make you call off the wedding?''

"Exactly what I told Mom,'' she insisted. "We
decided to wait for a while.''

"Then you're coming home?''

"Not right away. I'm still engaged. Just tell everybody to hold off on the wedding presents until
we set another date.''

"How long do you expect to stay there? You've
been gone for two weeks. Your money must be running out.''

"No, I have enough. You know what a good man-
ager I am.''

"That's not the way I remember it. If you're sure

you want to stay there for a while I'll send you some money.''

"No, Dad, I don't need any, honestly. I got a job over here. It pays more than enough to cover my expenses.''

Ben wasn't as naive as his daughter had been. "How could you get a job in a foreign country without a green card, or whatever they call their work permit? I'm sure they have the same stringent requirements we do. The formalities can take months.''

"I was lucky. I—'' Jillian paused.

She'd almost told him about meeting Gianni and how he'd come to her rescue, but that would only complicate matters further. Her father would be sure that Gianni was a decadent playboy whose real purpose was to seduce her. Better not to bring him into it at all.

"What sort of work do you do?'' Ben asked, with a hint of austerity in his voice.

"It's perfectly respectable. I'm not a go-go dancer or anything like that. Honestly, Dad, I would think you'd trust me to have a little common sense!''

"I have complete trust in you. I just want to know what kind of work you're doing.''

"I'm a secretary. There, is that respectable enough for you?''

"You got the position without papers?''

"Well...that's the best part.'' Jillian took a deep breath and gave the only explanation that occurred to her. "My fiancé offered me a job.''

"What you mean is, you're letting him support you." Ben's disapproval was transmitted across thousands of miles.

"No! It's a bona fide job. His secretary left to have a baby and he intended to hire someone anyway. Gianni is a very important man with a lot of business dealings."

"Who is Gianni? I thought you said your fiancé's name was Rinaldo."

"Oh…well, yes it is." That was an unpardonable slip! Could she get herself out of this one? "You see, Gianni is his middle name. All of his friends call him Gianni, and after I met them, I just started to call him that, too. It was less confusing when we were all together." Jillian held her breath, hoping he would buy that explanation.

"I'm not happy about this whole situation," Ben said slowly.

"Don't worry, Dad. I would never do anything to make you and Mother ashamed of me."

"I know you wouldn't, honey. I just can't help being concerned, even though I realize you're a grown woman. You'll understand when you're a parent yourself."

"I know what you're telling me. I love you, Dad," Jillian said in a husky voice.

"I love you, too, baby. Here, I'll let you talk to your mother. She'll rip the phone out of my hand if I don't give it to her soon." He handed the phone to his wife, saying, "She didn't marry the man, but she's working for him. Can you beat that?"

"You're working for Rinaldo?" Sarah asked as soon as she came on the line. "And who is Gianni? Did you meet somebody new?"

"Dad will give you the whole story. I have to go, Mom. I called you from work and I really should get off the phone."

"Of course, dear. I'll call you at the hotel. What time do you get back from work?"

"It's hard to say. Not until at least seven, or later if I stop someplace for dinner. Venetians keep different hours than we do."

"Then give me your office number and I'll call you there."

"I'll call *you* when I go out to lunch," Jillian said hastily. "I don't think I should receive personal calls on the job, even if I do work for my fiancé. It isn't businesslike."

"That's very commendable, but I'm sure Rinaldo wouldn't mind if your mother called just to say hello. I promise I'll be brief. Maybe I could even say hello to him, too," Sarah said in a casual voice. "We've never spoken to him."

"I'm sure he'd be thrilled to meet you." This was getting to be more painful than a root canal, Jillian thought.

"Good, then give me the number there."

Jillian had no choice. If she continued to refuse, they might begin to doubt her entire story.

After concluding the call, she hung up in numb disbelief at herself. Now her parents thought she was engaged to Gianni, only they thought he and Rinaldo

were the same person. It was like a French farce—
except that it wasn't funny! Considering how Gianni
felt about marriage, he'd be less than delighted to
hear that she was telling people they were engaged.
He wouldn't expose her if he found out, but he
might very well fire her!

How did she get into such predicaments? Jillian
put her head in her hands and stared down at the
desk.

Gianni appeared unexpectedly in the doorway.
"Is something wrong?" he asked.

"Oh!" She looked up, startled. "I thought you
were at your sister's."

"I haven't left yet. I got tied up with something.
Tell me what the problem is."

"There isn't one." Jillian smiled brightly. "Everything is going along just great."

"Did you call your parents?" he asked shrewdly.

"Yes, and you were right about getting it off my
mind. I feel a lot better."

"That wasn't the impression I got. Did they guess
why you called off the wedding?"

"No, but they asked a lot of questions."

"That's only normal."

"I guess so, but I felt badly about not telling them
the truth."

"It might have made you feel better—at least for
the moment—but it would only have upset them.
They would have been sure you had some more sin-
ister reason for not wanting to come home. Parents

continue to worry about their children, even after they're grown and out of the nest.''

Jillian smiled faintly. ''You must have met my parents.''

''They all have that trait in common.'' Gianni chuckled.

''Did your mother and father fuss over you, too?''

His smile vanished. ''It's hard to remember. My mother died when I was quite young.'' He looked at his watch. ''I'd better go. I'm late already.''

After he left, Jillian puzzled over Gianni's behavior. His whole manner had changed when she asked about his parents. Did he have a bad relationship with them—or perhaps only with his father? Gianni referred to him as little as possible.

But maybe he'd had a normal, loving family and she was just imagining problems that didn't exist. As Freud allegedly said, sometimes a cigar is just a cigar. It wasn't significant that he didn't talk about his father. The two of them might have been very close.

Gianni certainly seemed well-adjusted. And why not? He had everything a man could want—except a healthy attitude toward marriage. Jillian didn't envy the woman who fell hopelessly in love with him.

Chapter Four

Rinaldo was waiting in the lobby of Jillian's hotel when she returned from work that evening.

"*Cara mia,* at last!" he exclaimed. "The man at the desk said you were still registered here, but I was about to give up hope! I've been waiting hours for your return."

"How can you have the nerve to face me after that disgraceful scene in the church?" she exclaimed.

"We have to talk."

"What is there to say? I don't ever want to see you again."

"You can't mean that, my love. What happened that day was regrettable, and I'm willing to take all the blame. I'll admit that I should have told you about Maria, but I was afraid you would misunderstand. Our relationship was over long before I met you.''

''How about your relationship with your baby?''

''I will provide for the baby, naturally. I love children. You and I would make beautiful bambinos together,'' he said in a sensuous voice.

The voice she'd considered sexy, now sounded oily instead. She finally recognized the real Rinaldo, a liar and manipulator. The thought of him touching her made Jillian's flesh crawl. ''Go away, Rinaldo. It's over.''

''That's just your hurt pride talking, but I can make you forget the unpleasantness.'' He tried to take her hand, but she jerked it away. Unperturbed, he moved closer and said in a dulcet voice, ''Remember when we kissed in the shadow of the Ducal Palace late at night? All the plans we made for the future. They can still come true.''

Jillian shook her head, moving away. ''I was foolish enough to believe you once, but I'm not stupid enough to let you con me again.''

''Yet you're still here,'' he said softly. ''If you really didn't want to see me you would have gone home. Your vacation was over a couple of days ago.''

''Thanks to you I'm ashamed to go home!'' she said angrily. ''What would I tell my family and friends? That I called off the wedding because the mother of my bridegroom's child had first dibs on him?''

For an unguarded moment Rinaldo allowed his irritation to show. ''You act like I'm the only man who ever fathered a child out of wedlock. It happens!''

''Perhaps your next bride-to-be will be more understanding.'' Jillian stared at him searchingly, wanting to know the truth. ''Why did you ask me to marry you? And why did it have to be so quickly, before I had time to think things through? Was it because you thought I was rich?''

''How could you even imagine I was interested in your money? I would love you if you were penniless!'' Rinaldo declared passionately.

''I'm not destitute, but I'm not an heiress, either.''

He slanted a wary look at her. ''You told me your father owned a department store.''

''He does, but nothing like the big chain stores, if that's what you thought. My father makes a comfortable living, but Colby's is just a small, family-owned business.''

''It could be built into a moneymaker with the proper advice and marketing skills. I would be happy to offer my expertise, purely as a service to your family.'' He tried to sound casual, but the effect was marred by the glitter in his eyes.

She finally had her answer. Gianni was right about Rinaldo.

''We shouldn't be standing here like this. Let's

go up to your room and talk about us." He slid his hand up her arm.

She pulled away. "You've said enough. I'd like you to leave now."

"That's not what you really want," he said in a honeyed voice.

"Yes, it is. Leave me alone, Rinaldo. I've been gone since early this morning. I'm tired and I'm hungry."

"Then let me take you out to dinner, my love. We'll go to our place."

"We don't have a place. Unless you mean the corner trattoria we went to a few times. The one with the paper napkins."

"You said it had atmosphere."

"I was being polite." Jillian abruptly lost patience. "I'm not going to stand here arguing with you. If you don't leave this minute, I'll call a policeman and let *him* convince you that I mean business."

"You're not serious." He tried again to take her hand.

She brushed by him and marched over to the desk where a clerk had been watching them with interest. "Will you please call the police? This man is bothering me."

"Perhaps I can take care of the matter for you, signorina." The clerk was young and muscular.

As he came out from in back of the counter, Rinaldo started hastily for the door. "All right, I am going if that is your wish. But I will never give up hope. You are the love of my life!''

Jillian shook her head disgustedly. How could she have made allowances for all of Rinaldo's phony dramatics? All she felt now was relief that he was finally gone. When her eyes met the clerk's, he was trying not to laugh.

''I fear he will survive,'' the young man said.

''I'm sure of it. Thank you for your help.''

''Per niente.'' He shrugged, indicating thanks were unnecessary.

Jillian found her job so fascinating that she had no trouble putting Rinaldo out of her mind the next day. Her morning was taken up by conferences with hotel managers, the owner of a fleet of motor boats and a lighting expert. The ballroom would be turned into a medieval castle hall lit by flaming torches that would be powered by electricity, yet would look like the real thing.

Between meetings, she answered phone calls and made some of her own. She was amazed by the magic of Gianni's name. As soon as she said she was calling on behalf of the Duke of Venezia, she was put through immediately. It was a heady experience for someone used to waiting on the line endlessly, listening to canned music.

Gianni stopped by in the late morning to see how she was getting along. They talked about the ball for a few minutes, and then he said he had a business appointment.

"I'll take my pager in case you need me for anything. You can reach me on the Island of Murano."

"Is that where they make the famous Murano glass?"

He nodded. "Surely you've been there. It's on every tourist's list of things to do."

"I know, and I always wanted to go, but I just never got around to it."

"Why don't you come with me this morning? You can shop and see how they blow glass while I attend my meeting."

"I couldn't do that. I'm working."

"Since I'm your employer and it was my suggestion, you can consider it a work-related junket."

"When you put it that way, how can I refuse?" Jillian's cornflower-blue eyes shone in anticipation. She did want to see Murano and being with Gianni was always stimulating.

His motorboat was tied to one of the red-and-white-striped poles attached to the dock outside.

As they walked down the wooden planks leading to the sleek little craft, Jillian remarked, "Before I came to Venice I didn't see how a city could exist without automobiles. But it's a really civilized way of living. I love being able to walk down the middle of the street without having to dodge buses and taxicabs. It still seems strange, though, to get into a boat instead of a car when you want to go somewhere."

"That's part of the charm of Venice. We're unique."

"You won't get an argument from me." She glanced out over the busy canal. "I love it here!"

Gianni turned his head to gaze at the pure line of her profile. "We'll have to think of some way for you to stay."

Before she could answer, they reached the end of the dock where the motorboat was bobbing up and down in the wake of a passing *motoscafo*.

Gianni stepped into the boat first and held out his hand to her. "Watch your step. It's a little tricky when the big boats go by."

Jillian found that out. As she lifted her foot to step over the side, another ground swell caught her off balance.

Gianni's hands went to her waist, holding her to prevent her from falling. She gripped his shoulders to steady herself. Even as she teetered precariously, Jillian was aware of his superb physique. She could feel the muscles rippling in his broad shoulders, and the strength of the hands at her waist. Then Gianni lifted her into the boat and held her until he was sure she could stand alone.

"Sorry about that." She gave an embarrassed little laugh. "I'm not usually this clumsy."

"It wasn't your fault." He brushed a long strand of auburn hair out of her eyes. "It's happened to all of us."

Her cheek tingled where his fingers had trailed across it. She gazed into his eyes, feeling his magnetism wash over her.

Gianni's hands tightened around her waist for a

moment and his eyes took on a tawny glow. Jillian held her breath, feeling the mood between them change.

Then he released her and reached over to untie the boat. "I hope you won't mind wandering around Murano by yourself," he remarked.

"You needn't worry about me," she answered, a little breathlessly. "I never get tired of sightseeing."

"Maybe I can show you around a little. My appointment shouldn't take long."

"Do you have business interests on Murano?"

"No, my meeting is with an old friend who wants advice about his investments."

"You sound like an expert."

He shrugged. "I was tutored in finance at an early age. As the future head of the family, I would have to manage the di Destino estate."

"That must be a big job." Considering the size of their fortune, Jillian thought.

"Well, let's say it takes a lot of vigilance. I'm responsible for passing on the legacy to future generations, starting with my young nephews."

It was a perfect opening to ask about his family; he had brought up the subject. But before Jillian could question him, he was hailed by a friend in a passing boat. Then the traffic on the busy canal thickened as they approached Murano, and Gianni had to concentrate on maneuvering the speedboat to shore.

After they landed, he walked her to the main part of the little village and pointed out the glass factories and gift shops. They set a time to meet, and then he left her.

Jillian wandered around happily, taking in all the sights and sounds. She joined a group of people watching glass blowers create colorful vases and charming figurines, using a long pipe and a glob of molten glass.

The time flew by without her being aware of it. Gianni showed up at a store where she was admiring a display of exquisite paperweights.

"I knew if I went into enough gift shops I'd find you sooner or later." He chuckled.

She looked at her watch and gasped. "I'm so sorry! I completely forgot about the time."

"That means you were enjoying yourself."

"Oh, yes, I was! But I didn't mean to make you wait for me after you were nice enough to bring me here."

"I have nothing pressing to do now. Let's go have a drink. You must be ready to sit down after walking around for so long."

Gianni led her to a busy trattoria with umbrella tables outside. From their table they could watch the people strolling by and also enjoy a stunning view of the canal.

After Gianni had ordered wine for each of them, Jillian sighed happily. "It does feel good to sit down. Did you have a nice meeting with your friend?"

He shrugged. "We talked business, not very exciting."

"I thought that's what men liked to do—when they weren't talking about women," Jillian joked.

"That's a subject I'd much prefer." He returned her smile.

"You must know everything there is to know."

"What man ever does?" he said lightly. "Women are beautiful, mysterious creatures whose mission in life is to drive men mad."

"That's nice fiction, but men can aggravate women just as much."

Gianni looked amused. "It's called the battle of the sexes. And like most battles, the fighting eventually stops—unless the couple gets married."

Jillian looked at him curiously. "You're really down on marriage, aren't you? Did you have a disastrous one?"

"I wasn't speaking from experience. I've never been married."

"Then I don't understand your bias."

"It comes from observation—of my own family, as a matter of fact. I wouldn't mention it except that you're bound to meet my sister while you're here. She comes over constantly to complain about her husband. They're about as mismatched as two people can be. Angelina and Rudolfo have been married for ten years, and I swear they haven't spoken a civil word to each other for nine of them."

"Surely you're exaggerating. Maybe they're just volatile people who don't realize how they sound to others."

"I doubt very much if they care. They're too busy

trying to see who can exasperate the other more. I'm concerned about the effect it's having on the twins.''

"I suppose children do know when there is tension between their parents. Perhaps you could tactfully mention that to your sister.''

"I have, many times, but she refuses to admit it. She and Rudolfo alternate between overindulging the boys and ignoring them. It isn't surprising that they pay no attention to anything their parents tell them.''

"If things are really that bad perhaps they should consider getting a divorce,'' Jillian said.

"That isn't an option in our family.'' Gianni sat back in his chair and forced a smile. "I'm sorry. You must find this incredibly boring. I don't usually burden other people with my problems.''

"You let me tell you *my* troubles. You said I'd feel better afterward and I did.''

"It's a little different in my case. Normally I'm a very private person.''

"I know. This is the first time you've told me anything personal about yourself. At least now I understand why you're so anti-marriage.''

He looked amused. "I suppose that's the conclusion you would draw.''

"You mean I'm wrong? There's another reason?''

Gianni's smile didn't falter, but she got the impression that he was displeased. "Women are inveterate matchmakers. I think it's part of their genetic code.''

Which didn't answer her question. Jillian decided to back off. Maybe he'd had an unhappy love affair. It didn't seem possible that any woman would tire of him, but something must have happened. Whatever it was, he clearly didn't want to talk about it. That was confirmed when he changed the subject.

Gianni looked at the thin gold watch on his wrist. "Are you getting hungry? We could go to the Cipriani for lunch."

"I'd love that, but I'm afraid it would take too long," she said reluctantly. "I have to be back in the office by three for a meeting with the electrical technician. He wants to talk about some ideas he has for lighting the dock. We agreed that it should be something special."

"You're very conscientious."

"I told you I'd do a good job," she said.

"That doesn't include skipping lunch."

"Couldn't we eat here?"

"If you like." He signaled for a waiter.

Lunch was very pleasant, since Jillian didn't try to satisfy her curiosity about Gianni. It wouldn't have done any good, and it would only have alienated him. He didn't welcome intrusions into his private life. She'd just have to wait until he let something else slip and then try to put together the pieces of the puzzle.

Gianni was effortlessly charming, and so handsome that women passing by on the sidewalk turned their heads for a second glance. He was especially virile looking with his sable hair ruffled by the breeze off the water and his long, lean body relaxed in a chair.

"Do I have spaghetti sauce on my chin?" he asked when he noticed her staring at him.

"No, I was just thinking that you could be mistaken for a gondolier," she remarked. He was wearing tight-fitting jeans that emphasized his muscular thighs, and a black pullover that hugged his broad chest. "All you need is a bandanna around your neck."

"That's an idea for the ball. I'd certainly be comfortable dressed like this. Have you given any thought to your own costume?"

"You mean, you expect me to be there?" Jillian looked at him uncertainly. "My job will be over by then."

"I'm inviting you to be a guest. It should be amusing. Everybody will be trying to figure out who the masked mystery lady is."

"When the masks come off at midnight they'll still be wondering. Or are you planning to pass me off as royalty, the way Henry Higgins did with Eliza in *My Fair Lady*?"

Gianni smiled warmly. "You don't need to pretend to be anyone else. You're charming just the way you are."

Jillian was enormously pleased, even though she knew his friends wouldn't be as accepting. But she didn't expect to become part of his circle. Just being at the ball and seeing all the celebrities would be enough.

* * *

They arrived back at the villa with half an hour to spare. As Gianni was commenting on the fact, Marco informed him that his sister was waiting in the library.

Suddenly, two young boys dashed into the entry and launched themselves at Gianni with cries of delight. They weren't identical twins. One was a little taller than the other and their features were different, but they were both handsome children.

Gianni was laughingly fending them off. "Calm down, you two. You're acting like wild men. No wonder your mother can't handle you."

"Mamma didn't want to bring us today, but she had to. The nanny quit."

"What! Another one?" Gianni exclaimed.

"We're too old for a nanny anyway," one of the twins said.

"Besides, she was the worst of all," his brother declared. "She kept running to Mamma and telling on us."

"I don't even want to know what there was to tell." Gianni couldn't hide a grin.

Jillian was fascinated by this aspect of Gianni. The boys obviously adored him, and he returned their affection. What a wonderful father he would be. She had been watching them with interest until she realized she was intruding on a family moment. But as she started to leave, Gianni stopped her.

"I want you to meet my nephews before you go.

This is Joseph, and that's Roberto. Say hello to Signorina Colby.''

The boys were regarding her with lively speculation. ''Are you uncle Gianni's new girlfriend?'' Joseph asked.

''It isn't polite to ask personal questions,'' Gianni said.

''How else am I going to find out things?''

''You aren't. They don't concern you,'' his uncle said curtly.

''But we want to know what happened to Felicia.'' Roberto joined his brother's interrogation. ''You liked her a lot. You used to kiss her behind the ear when you thought we weren't looking.''

''That's enough!'' Gianni said.

The twins weren't daunted by his stern tone. ''Mamma didn't like her,'' Roberto continued. ''But Papa said he wouldn't mind trading places with you for a weekend. That's when Mamma got mad at him.''

''*Again!*'' the boys chorused, looking at each other and laughing.

Jillian wanted to join them. The look on Gianni's face was priceless. Two young boys had ruffled his poise as no woman ever could.

Gianni's jaw set as he took back control of the situation. He lowered his voice rather than raising it, which got the twins' attention. ''I don't want to hear another word out of either of you. We're going to have a talk about this later.''

The brothers avoided their uncle's eyes, looking concerned.

A tall, slender woman with glossy black hair came into the entry in time to hear Gianni's stern words to her sons. Angelina was young and beautiful, but her expression was sulky.

"What did they do now?" she asked.

"It isn't important," he answered.

"You don't want to admit they're a handful," she taunted. "You're always telling me it's all my fault when they misbehave."

"No, I give Rudolfo part of the credit," Gianni drawled.

"As though he ever has time for them," Angelina said scornfully. "*I'm* the one who loves them and worries about them!"

"Go into the other room," Gianni told the boys in a softer tone than he'd used earlier. He waited until they had left before saying to his sister, "Haven't you noticed that we're not alone? It's bad enough that you continually denigrate their father in front of the boys—unfortunately they're used to it. But do you have to air your dysfunctional relationship in front of a stranger?"

Jillian was acutely embarrassed. Why hadn't she gone directly to her office when they got back? But who could guess she'd get in the middle of a family argument? Gianni hadn't been exaggerating about his sister. Jillian didn't doubt that Angelina loved her children, but the woman seemed remarkably immature.

Knowing that Gianni must be embarrassed, too, Jillian sidled toward the door. "Well, I'd better get to work," she murmured.

His mouth curved sardonically. "I don't blame you. I can think of things *I'd* rather do, too."

"I'm sorry your family is such a burden to you." Angelina's voice dripped with sarcasm.

Gianni merely looked at her for a moment before saying to Jillian, "This is my sister, Angelina."

"It's nice to meet you," Jillian said politely.

After acknowledging the introduction, Angelina said, "Have you known my brother long?" She showed a little more tact than her sons, but she was just as curious.

"Jillian is filling in while Bella is on maternity leave," Gianni said.

"You aren't Italian," Angelina observed.

"It isn't a requirement for the job," he drawled.

"Honestly, Gianni, you criticize every word that comes out of my mouth!"

That was true, unfortunately. Angelina had only made an innocent remark, but any exchange between them provoked an argument. Jillian breathed a sigh of relief when Marco came to tell her the lighting specialist had arrived for their appointment.

The meeting took quite a while. Jillian walked around outside with the man and listened to his plans for loops of multicolored decorative lights around the dock, each garland centered perhaps with a candle shielded by a hurricane lamp.

After finishing their evaluation of the dock area, they went up to the ballroom and discussed those requirements. When all the workmen had done their jobs, the huge room would be reminiscent of the masked balls that royalty gave in the golden age of Venice.

Jillian was very excited about the preparations, but a little anxious about all the decisions she'd made. It would ease her mind if she could run them by Gianni while there was still time to make changes. Although, this wasn't the ideal moment. He was apt to be in a foul mood, even if his sister had left by now.

Jillian didn't have to worry about Gianni's mood. She discovered that he and his sister had both gone out, and Marco didn't know when Gianni would return. He'd left word that he wouldn't be home for dinner.

Jillian decided her questions could wait until tomorrow. The ball was still weeks away. She went into her office to catch up on all the work she hadn't done that afternoon.

When she noticed that her computer was turned on, she thought she'd forgotten to turn it off when she left with Gianni earlier. But Jillian distinctly remembered turning off the machine when she tidied up her desk. Then she saw there was gibberish on the screen. Letters and symbols, nothing that made sense.

"Please tell me it didn't develop a virus!" she begged out loud.

Part of the data she'd loaded was erased, but other entries weren't, which puzzled her. That wasn't the way a virus acted. Then it dawned on her—the twins! They'd been playing with her machine.

"Oh, no! Not my guest list. They couldn't have erased that!"

When she discovered they had, Jillian could have cried. She'd put in long hours making sure the list was accurate. Now it would have to be done over again without delay.

When guests sent regrets, their names were deleted from a list that would be checked at the door. For security reasons, no one would be admitted if their name wasn't on the list, regardless of whether or not they had one of the engraved invitations.

The women at the ball would be wearing a fortune in precious gems. They'd be a target for every jewel thief on the continent, if any of them could manage to breach security.

After muttering under her breath and slamming a few drawers, Jillian pulled out Bella's handwritten sheets of paper. Entering the names into the computer again was painstaking work. After a couple of hours her eyes were tired and her back ached, but she plodded on.

It was nearing eleven o'clock before the end was in sight. Jillian took a moment to stand and arch her tired back. She was startled when Gianni suddenly appeared in the doorway.

"What are you still doing here?" he exclaimed. "Do you know what time it is?"

"I...uh...I had some work to finish up." She didn't want to tell him what the twins had done. It wasn't really their fault. Nobody had ever laid down any rules for them.

"That's ridiculous! Whatever it was could have waited until tomorrow." He came around to look over her shoulder at the screen. "Is that the guest list you're working on? You told me you were finished with it."

"Well, yes, but the computer developed a little glitch." She gave him a weak smile. "I guess Bella was right about computers being undependable."

"Machines need servicing now and then, that's all. I'll call a repair man tomorrow."

"No, don't do that! I mean, I fixed it."

Gianni's eyes narrowed. "What's going on, Jillian? You're not telling me the truth—at least not all of it—and I want to know why."

She had no choice but to tell him what the twins had done. "They didn't realize they could mess things up. To them it was just an intriguing new toy."

"They had no right to be in here in the first place. Angelina should have kept track of them, but she was probably on the telephone, telling her troubles to anyone who would listen." He made an impatient gesture. "But you've heard enough about my family for one day. Did you have dinner?"

"No, but I'm not really hungry after that big lunch we had in Murano. I think I'll just go home. I'm almost caught up now."

"You can't skip dinner. I'll have one of the servants fix something for you."

"Thanks, but I'm more tired than I am hungry."

"I'm not going to let you walk alone at this hour. You'll stay here tonight. It's only sensible since it's so late now and you'll be coming back again in the morning."

Jillian was tempted. She used to think part of the charm of Venice was the absence of cars, cabs and buses. But a taxi sounded pretty good right now. Still, it wasn't the best idea.

"It's nice of you to offer, but I don't have a nightie, or even a toothbrush."

"I can offer you a toothbrush. I'm sure you can get by without a nightgown for one night."

Probably none of the women he knew ever wore one. Certainly not when they were with him, she thought cynically.

Gianni was reaching for a bellpull. "I'll have a room prepared for you. Decide what you want to eat."

He took it for granted that the matter was settled. Jillian decided to agree. It was easier than arguing with him. Gianni always got his own way anyhow.

Not that it would be a hardship to spend a night in a luxurious palazzo, Jillian thought with sudden anticipation. The fact that Gianni would be just down the hall added a little extra zing—for her anyway!

Chapter Five

Gianni had instructed Marco to bring Jillian's late supper to a small sitting room furnished informally with chintz sofas and chairs.

"I thought this would be cozier than the dining room," Gianni explained as he pulled out a chair for her. Eyeing the omelette that was all she'd requested, he asked, "Will that be enough for you?"

"More than enough," she assured him.

The omelette was garnished with sautéed mushrooms and broiled halves of tomatoes. A silver rack held toast, and several kinds of muffins were nestled in a basket. There were also crystal pots of marmalade and strawberry jam on the large silver tray.

"You don't have to sit with me," Jillian told him

as he took a seat opposite her at a gate leg table. "Are you afraid I won't clean my plate?" she joked.

"Somebody has to take care of you. Eat your eggs while they're hot." Gianni poured himself a cup of coffee from the silver pot that had accompanied her food.

Jillian glanced around the gracious room in between bites. "This is charming," she remarked. "I've never been in here before."

"It was my mother's favorite place. She used to read to me in this room. My fondest memories are of the times I spent in here, curled up on the couch next to her."

"This is an elegant house, yet it feels very warm," Jillian said.

"Yes, it's quite comfortable. I grew up here." He paused for so long that it was almost as if he'd forgotten she was there. Then he said, "Mother has been gone for a long time. She died in childbirth when I was seven."

"I'm so sorry," Jillian said in a muted voice. "That must have been terrible for you."

He nodded. "But at least I have wonderful memories of her. Angelina never knew her."

"That's really sad. It's hard to imagine never knowing your mother."

"I've always thought my sister might have turned out differently if she'd had Mother's gentling influence. Angelina was raised by a succession of nannies who let her do pretty much whatever she wanted because it was easier than trying to discipline her. She was strong-willed even as a little girl.''

''It would be difficult to say no to a motherless child.''

''I suppose so, and she was beautiful, as well. Angelina can also be very charming. She learned at an early age how to get her own way.''

''Didn't your father have any influence over her?''

Gianni's expression changed subtly. ''My father was always a very reserved man, and after Mother's death he withdrew even more. Angelina and I were raised basically by servants.''

''That's too bad. You could have been a great comfort to him.''

''He didn't let anybody get close to him, family or friends. I realize now that he blamed himself for inadvertently causing Mother's death. As a little boy, I resented him for not being there for us like she was. But as I grew older I understood what made him so disinterested. It wasn't anything personal. Without his wife, Father's life was meaningless.''

Jillian's heart twisted with pity for a lonely little boy. That could very well be the reason for Gianni's negative view of marriage. He didn't want to become emotionally dependent on another person, especially a woman. His father was an extreme case, but she could see how an impressionable child might be emotionally scarred. It was very sad. Gianni had led a privileged life. He'd been given every material thing, but not the most precious gift of all—love.

He smiled wryly at her. "I don't know why I'm telling you all this. It happened so long ago. Father died when I was in college."

"Sometimes we just feel like talking about things," she said in a casual tone, knowing he didn't want her pity.

"I have more pleasant memories of my childhood," he said in a lighter voice. "There was the time a friend and I stood outside the villa and charged tourists to go inside. Two couples walked in on the current nanny while she was taking a bath." Gianni laughed with remembered enjoyment. The brief glimpse into his psyche was over. "I forget her name because she wasn't with us very long."

"I don't blame her for quitting. You must have been a demon child."

"I suppose you're going to tell me you never did anything wrong."

"Of course I did, but I was careful not to get caught." She grinned.

They chatted together like old friends and the time flew by.

Finally Gianni looked at his watch and remarked, "I can't believe it's this late. You must be tired. I'll show you to your room."

Jillian was enjoying herself too much to care about the time, but she followed him upstairs.

After glancing around to be sure the room had been prepared properly, he opened the door to the bathroom. I think you'll find everything you need in here. I'll be back in a minute with a toothbrush and a robe.''

The bed had been turned down and the lamps were lit, which gave the room a welcoming look. Jillian was inspecting the bathroom when Gianni returned.

He handed her a new toothbrush and tossed the robe on the bed, saying with a smile, ''This should make you feel right at home. It still has the scent of your perfume on it.''

She was reminded of their traumatic meeting, but surprisingly, the thought of Rinaldo no longer upset her. Was it because she wouldn't have met Gianni if it hadn't been for her bad experience with Rinaldo? Not that Gianni would ever play a significant part in her life, but just getting to know him was a rare treat.

''I hope you'll be comfortable here,'' he said. ''If you need anything, just ring for one of the servants.''

After Gianni left, Jillian undressed and hung her clothes in the closet before going into the bathroom to brush her teeth and take a shower. The bathroom had been modernized to include every sort of gadget. A hair dryer hung on the wall next to a round mirror on a flexible arm, and thick, monogrammed towels were draped over heated towel rods. Over the sink was a row of buttons whose functions were a mystery.

After pressing all of them Jillian discovered that one button lit bright lights over the sink, another turned on a fan to dispel any moisture on the mirror. The third button didn't seem to serve any purpose that was evident.

She spent a few more moments looking for a shower cap, which she found tucked into a basket of toiletries—cologne spray, body lotion and shampoo. Just like in a luxury hotel, except these were generous bottles, not little sample sizes. As she was about to turn on the shower, Jillian remembered the robe still lying on the bed. She opened the bathroom door and walked naked into the bedroom.

It was a toss-up as to who was more startled when they met face-to-face, Jillian or Gianni. His surprised expression changed to sensuous appreciation as his avid glance moved over her slender, nude body like a caress.

For an instant, Jillian felt an answering flash of the desire so obvious in his golden eyes. Her body responded automatically to Gianni's potent masculinity.

Then sanity returned, and she raced over to grab the robe off the bed and hold it against her body to shield herself. "What are you doing here?" she demanded. "I didn't know I had to lock the door to keep you out. Or does it even have a lock?"

"I'm sorry," he murmured in a bemused voice.

Mamma mia, the woman had the body of Circe, the seductress! How he would love to take her in his arms and kiss her everywhere. Gianni forced himself to concentrate on her face, which didn't lessen his desire. Her softly curved mouth drew him like a magnet.

"You're sorry? That's no explanation!" she flared. "What gives you the right to just walk in on somebody without knocking?"

"I did knock, but you didn't hear me. I realized you must be in the bathroom with the door closed. I was about to knock on the bathroom door when you came out unexpectedly."

"I forgot my robe—but that doesn't excuse this intrusion! Why did you come back?"

"To give you whatever you wanted."

Her temper exploded. "You are without a doubt the worst male chauvinist I've ever encountered! What makes you think I want anything from you?"

"You rang your call bell."

Jillian stared at him with sudden comprehension. That last button she'd pushed in the bathroom must be to summon a servant! Her cheeks turned the color of wild roses.

"Marco was coming to find out what you needed, but I told him I'd take care of it," Gianni explained.

"I wondered what all those buttons were for, so I tried all of them," she mumbled.

"I suppose they should be labeled. It isn't the first time something like this has happened."

Jillian doubted that. Or if it had, she'd bet no other guest had overreacted so badly. "I'm sorry," she murmured. "I should have known you wouldn't do a thing like this intentionally."

His eyes twinkled with merriment. "It's not

something a gentleman does,'' he agreed. ''But that doesn't mean I'm not grateful for the mishap. You have nothing to be embarrassed about.'' Gianni moved to the door before she could react. ''Sleep well.'' He closed the door softly.

After he was gone Jillian sank down on the bed and groaned, remembering the dreadful things she'd said to him. Anybody with a grain of sense would have realized that Gianni didn't have to ambush a woman. Finding willing bed partners would be no problem for him.

What bothered her wasn't the fact that he had seen her naked. She was sure he'd seen more than his share of nude women. What concerned Jillian was her own reaction to him. For one wild moment she'd wanted to throw her arms around his neck and pull his head down so she could feel his mouth moving over hers. What on earth had come over her? Gianni was a handsome, virile man, yet she'd never felt such a primitive urge before.

The problem now was concealing that fact from him. She'd have to be constantly on guard because he was very knowledgeable about women. Jillian sighed as she went into the bathroom once more. Facing Gianni tomorrow was going to be pure hell!

Jillian was up very early the next morning. The picturesque, winding streets were free of tourists for once, as she walked back to the hotel for a change of clothes.

She never wore tight T-shirts or anything overtly

sexy, but that morning her choice was consciously conservative, a pleated skirt and a blouse with a high neck. She wanted to project the most businesslike image possible.

As she walked back to Gianni's villa, Jillian thought about how she should act when they met. She could refer to last night's mishap with amusement. That might be difficult, though, given her annoying tendency to blush. Maybe it would be better to simply pretend the incident hadn't happened.

All the thought she'd devoted to their initial meeting turned out to be wasted. Gianni didn't come near the office that morning as he usually did. Jillian tensed at every footstep in the hall, but noon came and Gianni didn't. He was probably trying to spare her discomfort, she decided. Surprisingly, her relief was mixed with regret. Gianni was always stimulating company, even when he disturbed her equilibrium.

By late afternoon, Jillian no longer expected him to stop by. She was deep in thought as she stood in front of the file cabinet, searching through the manila folders for the caterer's estimate. Gianni's deep voice startled her. She whirled around to find him standing in the doorway.

"You look like a French schoolgirl," he remarked with a smile. "All you need is a boater hat with streamers down the back."

Everything she'd planned to say deserted her. "I think the caterer is padding his bill," she said abruptly.

"Probably." Gianni strolled over and took the chair in front of the desk. "It's what I believe you Americans call a perk."

"That's unacceptable! He's making a profit on the food, and you'll undoubtedly tip him. I'm going to call him on it."

"Don't do that. He's the best caterer in Venice. If he gets angry and quits, you'll have to make hors d'oeuvres for six hundred people," Gianni teased.

"I'm serious about this. I know the money doesn't mean anything to you, but it's the principle of the thing. The man is taking advantage of you!"

"All right, I'll speak to him." He changed the subject to distract her. "You were out very early this morning. Marco told me what time you left."

"I had to go back to the hotel to change clothes."

"You could have started work a little later."

"I was up anyway." Jillian shuffled through some papers on her desk and handed him a sheaf of messages. "These are the people who called today. Most of them want you to call them back. Several of the slips are from the Countess of Rivoli. She phoned three times, but she wouldn't leave a message. She just said she had to talk to you."

The woman had been very insistent. Jillian was curious to know what Gianni's relationship with the countess was. Her voice sounded young, not like the Countess of Albion's. But he took the slips of paper without comment.

"Were there any crises while I was out?" he asked.

"No, just business as usual." She concentrated on stacking some papers in a precise pile. Why couldn't she be as relaxed with him as she used to be?

Gianni's eyes lit with mischief as he gazed at her bowed head. "I had hoped that last night's little incident would be forgotten this morning, but I can see that it's still bothering you. I believe I have a solution. Do you think we can be friends again if I take off my clothes and let you see *me* in the nude?"

Jillian couldn't help laughing. Instead of avoiding the subject as she had, he'd put last night's happening into its proper perspective. It was no big deal.

"Thanks for the offer," she said. "But if you don't mind, I'll take a rain check. I need to get your opinion on something concerning the ball."

"My offer has no expiration date. What did you want to talk about?"

"Security, for one thing. Do you want the guards dressed in costume? They could mingle with the crowd unobtrusively that way. On the other hand, would it be a preventive measure if the guards were identifiable? Not in uniforms, of course—perhaps in dinner jackets."

"I realize security is necessary, but I don't want my guests to feel as if they're under surveillance," Gianni said. "Let's explore all of the possibilities."

They discussed that and some of the other preparations necessary for such a lavish party. The days seemed to be flying by. Jillian had been looking forward to the ball with great anticipation, but now that the big night was not too distant, her feelings were mixed.

She would have no reason to remain in Venice after the ball. Or more accurately, she couldn't afford to. The job with Gianni had made her extended stay possible, but he wouldn't need her once the ball was over, and she couldn't get another job.

Jillian sighed. This time there would be no miracle solution to her problem. She'd just have to enjoy every minute of the time that was left.

"Jillian?" Gianni was looking at her quizzically.

She realized he had asked her a question. "I'm sorry. I guess my mind was wandering. You were saying something about the costumes?"

"We don't have to decide that right now. Your brain has gone into overload. Come on, let's go to Harry's Bar for a drink. You need to take a break."

She looked doubtfully at her cluttered desk. "I still have a few things to do here."

"I'm sure they can wait until tomorrow."

Jillian decided he was right. Harry's Bar was a well-known landmark in Venice. She'd always wanted to go there, but Rinaldo told her it was a tourist trap. That was his excuse whenever he didn't want to spend money, she realized now.

Gianni was evidently a regular at the famous bar. The bartender and the waiter who came to take their order greeted him by name.

When Jillian commented on the fact after the man had left to get their drinks, Gianni said, "Venice is really a small town. If you lived here for any length of time you would get to know everyone, too."

"That would be nice," she said wistfully. "I've caught glimpses of that small-town atmosphere. Like seeing the local women carrying their baskets from stall to stall in the open air market. They have long conversations with the clerks over which melon is ripe, or whether the eggs were freshly laid."

Gianni smiled. "Food is a serious subject to an Italian."

"Marketing seems like fun here. At the supermarkets in California we never see a butcher or a produce clerk, much less talk to one. Everything is wrapped in plastic and stacked in cases. You pick out what you want and take it to the checkout stand."

"That sounds very sterile."

"It is. That's why grocery shopping at home is a chore rather than a pleasure."

"Do you like to cook?" he asked.

"Yes, it's one of my hobbies. I'd attempt to make some of the Italian dishes I've tried here if I had access to a kitchen."

"I'd offer to let you use mine, but the cook might quit. She's very temperamental."

Jillian smiled. "I wouldn't want you to lose a good cook on my account. You can replace me more easily than her."

"Don't underestimate yourself," Gianni said softly. "I'm becoming very dependent on you."

She knew he was just being gallant, but the light

in his eyes as he gazed at her across the small table made her glow like a sunset.

"I've tasted Gina's cooking," Jillian said, managing a small laugh. "I couldn't take her place—although it would mean I could stay in Venice longer."

"Are you tired of your present position?"

"Not at all! But it's a temporary job. Your secretary will be back sooner or later."

"That's true." Gianni looked at her speculatively. "Would you like to live in Venice?"

"You mean permanently? I hadn't thought about it, but I would like to spend the rest of the summer here."

"Maybe that can be arranged."

"I doubt if you need two secretaries." She had no intention of accepting charity, no matter how well meant.

"Well, we'll see. You really should move to a little apartment, for however long you're here. It must be awfully cramped living in one room. You could get a bigger place for the same amount of money, or perhaps even less."

"My hotel isn't that expensive. They gave me a better rate when I told them I was staying on for an extended period. And I don't spend much time in my room. It's really quite adequate."

"If you say so," he said with obvious disbelief.

She took a sip of the drink the waiter had brought and changed the subject. "This Bellini cocktail you recommended is delicious. What's in it?"

"Mostly peach juice. I thought you should try it. The Bellini is as synonymous with Venice as the Sazerac cocktail is with New Orleans."

"A lot of places seem to have a signature drink."

"Or a fancy presentation. Like those oversize drinks with fruit and paper parasols you get in Polynesian-type restaurants."

"I used to have a collection of those little parasols," Jillian said. "Each one reminded me of a special event, and the boyfriend I fancied myself in love with at the time."

"You must have gone out with a lot of men," he said, gazing at her delicate features framed by long, shining hair. "Wasn't there ever one special man?"

She smiled wryly. "That's the sort of question that made me run away to Venice. I'm sure you're asked the same thing by your friends and family."

His answering smile was cynical. "Yes, people want the whole world to be one gigantic Noah's Ark. They think all adults should be paired off, two by two."

"Is that so terrible?"

He shrugged. "No, if it's what you want. But not everybody needs another person to be complete."

So she was right! Jillian thought. His father's example *was* responsible for Gianni's fear of commitment.

"Still, it must be nice to have somebody who cares about you," she said in a casual voice.

"Have you ever considered getting a dog?" he teased.

She realized that any serious conversation between them was over. Gianni was like a wild stallion. He didn't permit anyone to get too close.

The conversation drifted to other things, and all traces of his cynical mood disappeared. Jillian hoped he would ask her to have dinner with him. But when she saw him slant a surreptitious peek at his watch she knew he probably had a date.

"Well, I have to be going," she said. "Thanks for bringing me here. I really enjoyed it."

"I did, too. We must do it again." He took out some bills and signaled for the check.

They went in different directions when they got outside.

Jillian usually enjoyed the walk to the hotel after work. She looked in shop windows and watched the people of every nationality having coffee and chatting at little sidewalk tables. Then she stopped in some bustling trattoria for a plate of pasta or risotto, better than any she'd ever eaten at home.

But that night she was too distracted by thoughts of Gianni to follow her normal routine. Who did he have a date with? Somebody glamorous, no doubt. The imperious countess Sylvie, who called regularly?

What difference did it make? Gianni's personal life didn't matter to her, Jillian told herself in annoyance. He was wildly attractive, but it wasn't as if she was falling in love with him. That would be really dumb!

She started to walk faster, reviewing all the things she had to do. There was never much time for them after she got back from work. Tonight she simply must write to her parents; that was a top priority. They worried if they didn't hear from her regularly and she'd been putting it off for too long.

The letters were difficult to write because she still felt guilty at deceiving them about her relationship with Gianni. She'd made everything about him sound so perfect that it would be difficult to explain, when the time came, why they'd broken up.

Her letters mentioned how much she loved her job. She'd described his palazzo in detail, the opulent furnishings, the many servants that kept the vast house spotless.

"There are so many bedrooms that it could double as a hotel," she'd written.

In earlier letters she'd described Gianni, his laughing, tawny eyes, the way his dark hair looked when it was tousled by the wind off the canals.

"I don't know which are more impressive, his aristocratic features or his stunning physique."

Then later she'd mentioned how sophisticated he was, yet how thoughtful and caring.

Well, she hadn't really lied to her parents, Jillian reasoned as she pushed open the door to her hotel. All of those things were true. She'd only told one outright lie—and it was a whopper! Gianni was her employer, not her fiancé.

Chapter Six

The next morning, Gianni received a phone call from Enrico. "I have that information you wanted on Rinaldo Marsala. He's a really sleazy character."

"I'd already formed that opinion," Gianni said. "Do you have actual proof?"

"Nothing that would stand up in court. He's very street-smart. The police have had some complaints about him, but they've never been able to make anything stick. He romances female tourists—young or old, it doesn't matter—but that isn't against the law. After they think they're in love with him, he sweet talks them out of their money, using a variety of different scams."

"Surely *that's* illegal."

"Only if you can prove it. The police brought him in for questioning a couple of times, but Marsala said the money was a gift. It was the victim's word against his—and maybe part of the time he was telling the truth. He's said to be a Latin-lover type, the sort that appeals to the ladies."

"So his only crime is making love to gullible women and accepting payment for it? Or tricking them into giving it to him."

Gianni was beginning to regret the things he'd told Jillian about Rinaldo's darker motives for wanting to marry her. The man had the ethics of a snake, but maybe he was really in love with her.

"Marsala is known for being a small-time con man, but recently he expanded his horizons, so to speak," Enrico said. "When he attracted a woman who was rich enough, he went for the gold and proposed to her."

Gianni's doubts started to dissipate. Jillian was luckier than she knew. The man might be a bigamist. "Did any of them actually marry him?"

"Just one that we know about, although he got close a couple of times. They were well-to-do widows whose children broke up the romance. The one he succeeded in marrying was a French schoolgirl from a wealthy family. Her father had the marriage annulled, and then had to pay Marsala to stop contacting her. The man is a real leech."

"Are women his only source of support?" Gianni asked.

"As far as we can judge. He's never held a job

here in Venice. There are always tourists in town for him to prey on. One scam that he uses often is particularly successful.''

"Don't tell me what it is," Gianni said with distaste, "I've heard enough."

"All right, I'll just mail you the report. You can read it when your stomach settles."

Gianni hung up slowly. None of what he'd just heard surprised him. He had intended to show the report to Jillian as a cautionary measure, because she'd found it difficult to believe Rinaldo could be that contemptible. This would convince her, but it would also damage her self-esteem—the last thing Gianni wanted to do. Jillian didn't need to know the report existed.

She found out on her own when the mail was delivered to her office the next morning. There were always a lot of letters, business correspondence mixed in with the party replies. Occasionally there were notes marked "personal." She put those aside unopened. They were probably from women, she guessed, judging by the flowery handwriting.

The report on Rinaldo came in a business envelope, with Gianni's name and address typed, not written by hand. Jillian opened the envelope routinely. She was puzzled at first when her eye caught Rinaldo's name. By the time she finished reading the report, her body was taut.

Gianni came in while she was staring at the sheets

of paper clutched in her hand. His smile dimmed. "Is something wrong?"

She looked at him without expression. "Why did you have Rinaldo investigated?"

"Is that the report?" He swore under his breath. "Enrico should have had sense enough to mark it private and confidential. You weren't supposed to see that."

"Then what was the purpose?"

"It wasn't merely prurient curiosity. I wanted to know what kind of a man he was, in case he tried to contact you again."

"Wasn't it obvious after the things I told you?" she asked.

"It was to me, but you found it difficult to believe he could be as devious as I painted him."

"You thought Rinaldo could talk me into going back to him?"

Gianni hesitated, wanting to justify himself without hurting her in the process. "Fortunately you've never met anyone like him. Men like Rinaldo prey on decent people, using their victims' inexperience to their own advantage. I didn't want you to get hurt again. I apologize if I was out of line."

Jillian couldn't believe that someone like Gianni would take the time and trouble to protect her from making another mistake. "I think what you did was extraordinarily kind," she said in a husky voice.

"Oh well, we all have to look out for each other. That's what it's all about." He shrugged, minimizing his effort, then changed the subject. "I brought you another couple of names to add to the guest list.''

''We're going to need a shoehorn to get them all in,'' she commented.

After Gianni left, Jillian couldn't stop thinking about him. What an extraordinary person he was to be so solicitous of someone who meant nothing to him. She was almost starting to wish his interest in her *was* personal—although that was impossible. They came from different worlds.

In the days that followed, Gianni got into the habit of dropping by Jillian's office in the late afternoon. They discussed the ball and any problems that might have arisen, and then they just chatted about things that had happened during the day.

Jillian began to look forward to this time with him. She was a little disappointed that Gianni didn't ask her out again, but it was probably for the best. Neither of them wanted to get involved.

She had to remind herself of that fact when she stayed past her usual quitting time one night and happened to see Gianni walking down the hall. Most men looked their best in evening clothes, but he looked spectacular! The well-tailored black dinner jacket emphasized his height and the width of his broad shoulders, while his snowy white shirt provided a stunning contrast to his deeply tanned face.

He did a double take when he saw Jillian sitting at her desk. ''What are you still doing here? You should have gone home an hour ago.''

"I'm waiting for a reply to a fax I sent." She looked at him with open admiration. "You look smashing! Big night tonight?"

Gianni shrugged. "It's a charity affair. One of those good causes you can't turn down."

"Why would you want to? Everybody will be all dressed up and in a party mood. I'll bet it's going to be one of those glittering events I'll read about in the paper tomorrow morning."

She looked like a little girl gazing through a candy store window. "I would have gotten you an invitation if I'd thought you wanted to go," he said. "But these things aren't really that much fun. You have to sit through a lot of speeches and the dinner is only so-so."

"I wonder why men never enjoy parties as much as women do. But I wasn't hinting that I wanted to go. I wouldn't know anybody there."

The doorbell rang in the entry hall. Then several male and female voices drifted down the hall after Marco answered the door.

Gianni hesitated. "I feel like a slave driver, going out and leaving you working here all alone."

"This is my job. Your job is to look glamorous and be photographed with the rest of the beautiful people."

He gave her a look that was part amusement, part annoyance. "Is that what you think my life is like?"

"Don't knock it," she teased. "A large section of the population would be glad to change places with you."

Before he could answer, a woman's lilting voice called out, "Gianni darling, where are you? We're all here and ready to party."

Jillian recognized the countess's voice. The woman had called often enough! Finally she'd get a look at her.

Gianni started for the door. "I'd better go. I'm taking everyone in my boat."

Sylvie, the Countess of Rivoli, appeared at the door. She was very beautiful and very glamorous. Her blond hair was artfully styled, and the magnificent emerald necklace around her smooth throat matched the emerald green of her eyes.

"What are you doing back here?" she asked Gianni, without noticing that he wasn't alone. "Aren't you ready?"

"Yes, I was just talking to Jillian for a moment. I believe you've spoken to each other on the phone." He introduced the two women.

Sylvie's smile wasn't reflected in her eyes as they assessed Jillian. "Oh, yes, you're the one who won't ever let me talk to Gianni."

"I can never find him myself," Jillian answered blandly.

"Is that the fax you're waiting for?" he asked as the machine on a corner table started to whirr. "Now you can go home. You've done enough for today."

After the glamorous couple had left, Jillian wondered just how close their relationship was. The countess's possessive manner gave the impression that they were serious about each other, but knowing Gianni's fear of commitment, Jillian didn't think it was going to lead to anything permanent.

He was very charming, though. She could imagine him holding Sylvie's hand as he helped her in and out of the boat, his head dipping toward hers as he murmured some laughing comment. And then later that night when he and the countess were alone together, the glow in his eyes as he slid an arm around her waist and drew her against his hard body.

Jillian pushed back her chair abruptly and got to her feet.

Gianni was so adept at the social graces that none of his friends, not even Sylvie, realized he wasn't giving them his full attention. She would have been furious if she'd known that while she was being discreetly seductive, his mind was occupied with Jillian.

She'd looked so wistful, he thought, like a little girl who was the only one who wasn't going to the party. He knew how much Jillian enjoyed what she considered *la dolce vita*—even simply having a drink at a famous bar. So why hadn't he invited her to tonight's party, a formal affair in a grand *palazzo*?

Her delight would have made a routine social event something special for him, as well. And that was the dilemma. The strong physical attraction between them was a little troubling. He found himself thinking about her during the day, wanting to be with her more and more.

Ordinarily that wouldn't have been a problem. Gianni was experienced enough to know that Jillian was attracted to him, too. If she were any other woman, they could have had a highly enjoyable affair. They would have kissed in a gondola and perhaps danced in the secluded side garden in the moonlight. Then they might have undressed each other slowly and resumed their dance until their passion demanded fulfillment right there on the soft grass.

But Jillian wasn't like the women he knew. He could bet that she didn't make love lightly, for the mere pleasure involved. She would expect—if not marriage—at least some solemn commitment, some tie that would be more than physical. And that was something he couldn't give. It was the reason he tried not to involve her in his personal life. For her sake as well as his own.

Then he thought of the naive pleasure she derived out of the small things he took for granted, and Gianni was ashamed of himself. Yes, Jillian was adorable, and he wanted to make love to her, but he was neither a hormonally challenged teenager, nor romantically deprived. They could be friends instead of lovers. It should be an interesting experience, he told himself wryly.

Gianni showed up in Jillian's office earlier than usual the next day. Before she could question him about the party the night before, he surprised her by saying he had a favor to ask.

"Of course," she said. It was the first time he'd ever asked her for anything. "What can I do for you?"

"If you're free this evening, I'd like you to attend a dinner party with me."

She was too surprised to answer for a moment This was different than a casual lunch or a drink after work.

"I know it's last minute," he said, "but my date came down with the flu. It's just a small dinner party, six or seven couples. It would spoil the hostess's seating arrangement if I came alone."

Jillian was as wary as Gianni of becoming overly friendly—and for at least one of the same reasons. She was too attracted to him. But this wasn't a date, it was a favor, which she certainly owed him. "I'd love to go with you!" she said, her face lighting up.

"Splendid! I'll just tell Sophia to change the names on the place cards."

"Are you sure she won't mind that you're bringing a total stranger?"

"She'll be delighted to have you. You'll like Sophia and Dino. The three of us have been friends since college days, before she and Dino were married. They have two adorable little daughters. I'm their godfather."

Gianni was certainly involved with other people's children. Maybe that's why he didn't feel the need to have any of his own, Jillian decided.

"Why don't you go to your hotel and bring back a change of clothes for tonight? It will be a lot easier if we leave from here. The Antonettis live just down the Grand Canal from my place.''

Jillian's hotel wasn't on a canal, so it didn't have a boat dock, which meant she had to walk everyplace she needed to go. The large palazzos like Gianni's had private docks.

"You can plan to stay here overnight," he continued. "I doubt if you'll feel like walking back to the hotel after the party."

Jillian grinned. "You mean, *you* won't feel like walking me home."

"That, too." He chuckled. "Take one of the servants if you need help carrying your things back here."

Something occurred to her. "What was I thinking? I can't go tonight. I have nothing to wear!"

"I'm sure you can find something. You always look lovely."

"I don't have anything suitable to wear to a party. I saw the way the countess was dressed last night." She'd had on a stunning, strapless white satin gown, and of course those glorious emeralds.

"That was a formal affair, this is just a small dinner party."

"But I'm sure everybody will be dressed beautifully, and I really don't have anything adequate. I wouldn't want to disgrace you or myself."

"My dear Jillian, you're being foolish." He gave her a baffled look. "You must have something you'd feel comfortable in. How about that pretty white dress you were wearing the day we met?"

"My wedding gown? I'd never wear that thing again! I should have thrown it away after what happened. I don't know why I didn't." Probably because it had been so expensive.

"I didn't realize Rinaldo could still upset you to this extent. You haven't mentioned him recently."

"I never think about him anymore," she answered truthfully. Rinaldo had been a painful experience, but Jillian was more embarrassed by her lack of good judgment than anything else.

Gianni shrugged. "If Rinaldo is history, the dress has no significance. You can throw it out if you like, or you can wear it and move on with your life."

That made sense. After all, she'd been wearing the dress when she met Gianni, and look how that turned out!

Jillian's arms were full when she returned from the hotel. Besides her outfit for that evening, she'd brought nightclothes and something to wear the next day. It would probably be late when they got back from the party, and she wouldn't have to get up as early if she had a change of clothes right there at Gianni's.

As she hung her things in the closet of the same room she'd occupied before, Jillian couldn't help being reminded of the night Gianni had surprised her in the nude.

A little shiver ran up her spine as she recalled the smoldering look on his face. For one quivering moment she'd thought he was going to take her in his arms. What would the outcome have been? She had to admit that part of her had wanted to feel his seductive hands moving over her body, his warm mouth trailing a line of kisses where his hands had visited.

Jillian took a deep breath to banish the disturbing vision. Something like that would never happen again, she assured herself. But just to make sure, she locked the bathroom door securely when she went to take a shower.

Gianni might have had the same reservations about coming to her room. He called her on the house phone later that evening to ask her to join him in the downstairs den when she was ready.

Jillian took a last moment to check her appearance. She had thrown a pale blue cardigan around her shoulders and added a necklace of aquamarine crystal beads so her white dress wouldn't resemble a wedding gown. The shades of blue accentuated the color of her eyes and made a nice contrast with her dress.

Gianni was having a drink and glancing at the evening paper when Jillian joined him. His desultory gaze turned to admiration when he glanced up and saw her. "You look lovely." His eyes roved over her creamy skin and sweetly curved mouth. "Has anyone ever told you that you're a very pretty young woman?"

She gave a bubbly little laugh. "My parents tell people that, but they're prejudiced. It's always more gratifying when a compliment comes from a stranger.''

''You can't consider me a stranger after we've practically been living together.''

''That sounds a lot racier than it is.''

''Unfortunately you're right.'' He chuckled as he put a companionable arm around her shoulders and led her to the entry.

Gianni had set just the right tone, Jillian thought. There was a definite sexual attraction present between them, but they were adults. They could handle it.

The other guests were already present when Jillian and Gianni arrived at the gracious palazzo near his. Welcoming light shone out of the tall windows of the formal drawing room, creating wavering golden ribbons on the dark water of the canal. While they waited for a butler to open the door, Jillian could see a waiter circulating among elegantly dressed guests as he refilled their champagne glasses. It was almost like a scene from a play, but these people actually lived this way, she thought happily.

Everyone was very friendly, and too well-bred to ask questions, although they were clearly curious about Jillian. She supposed that any new woman Gianni appeared with was subject to the same intense speculation. His friends didn't realize that nothing lasting was going to come of any of his romances—or that she and Gianni weren't even romantically involved.

"I'm so glad you could join us tonight," Sophia told Jillian. She was a stunning, very outgoing woman. "Gianni is one of our favorite people."

"Both of our girls want to marry him when they grow up," Dino, Sophia's husband, remarked.

"Maybe by then his reflexes will be slower and one of them will be able to catch him," a male guest laughed.

"Leave Gianni alone," Sophia said, after a look at his set smile. "He mentioned that you're from the States," she said to Jillian, changing the subject. "Dino and I were in New York last month. We had a perfectly marvelous time."

They talked about America for a bit. Everyone had visited there at one time or another. Then Gianni told them Jillian was coordinating the ball for him.

"You poor thing!" a woman named Antonia exclaimed. "What a lot of work!"

"I'm enjoying it," Jillian said.

"Dealing with all those massive egos? And I don't mean the caterer and his crew. It must be a logistical nightmare getting accommodations for a horde of demanding people. You can't please some of them no matter what you do."

"That's easy compared to pacifying the ones who are sure their invitation got lost in the mail," another woman said. "How do you tell them they weren't invited? That's social suicide!"

"With so many people on the list, I don't see how

anybody could possibly have been left out,'' Jillian commented.

''Brace yourself! You'll hear from every one of them.''

''Maybe some invitations really did get lost. I'll check to see if they're right.''

Sophia looked at Gianni with a raised eyebrow. ''Does she also believe the Easter Bunny lays chocolate eggs?''

''Probably.'' He grinned. ''Where everybody else sees weeds, Jillian sees wildflowers.''

''Hang on to that girl,'' Dino advised. ''Her kind is rarer than rubies.''

''I know,'' Gianni said softly.

Dinner was served soon after that in the dining room, where they were all seated at a long polished table lit by candles in tall silver holders. The china was exquisite, and a series of crystal goblets was lined up at every place setting. A different wine was served with each course.

But as elegant as all that was, Jillian was most impressed by the conversation. It ranged from art to politics to socially conscious concerns, sparking spirited discussions. These were intelligent, charming people who couldn't be friendlier. She was having a wonderful time, and her delight showed on her face. Gianni watched her with a bemused expression, but for once she wasn't aware of him.

After dinner they all went back to the drawing room. This time, though, the men congregated at one end of the long room while the women gathered on a couple of couches at the other end. The ball was mentioned again and they discussed what they planned to wear. That's how Sylvie's name came up.

"She won't give even a hint about her costume, but I'll bet it will be something eye-popping," Antonia said.

"Sylvie tried to get Gianni to come as King Louis XVI so she could be Marie Antoinette," Sophia said. "But she couldn't convince him."

"Can you imagine Gianni in a powdered wig and satin shoes with fancy heels?" another woman hooted.

"He's one of the few men who could carry it off with style. What *is* he wearing?" Antonia asked Jillian.

"I don't know that he's decided yet."

"Really?" They all looked at her skeptically.

"Honestly. You know more about it than I do. I didn't even know the countess was his date for the ball." Jillian wasn't delighted to hear it. Not that it mattered to her, but Gianni was such a nice person. He deserved somebody with more warmth.

"She isn't his date," Sophia said. "Sylvie has been giving everybody the impression that she is Gianni's hostess for the evening, but it's only wishful thinking on her part. He wouldn't choose her."

"He took her to that charity affair last night." Jillian tried to make her comment sound casual.

"That doesn't mean anything. Gianni is amazing.

He manages to stay on good terms with all his former women friends.''

"Don't count Sylvie out," Antonia said. "She doesn't give up easily when she wants something, and Gianni has been at the top of her wish list for years.''

One of the other women slanted an uncomfortable look at Jillian. "I don't think this is the most tactful conversation we could be having. Jillian must know Gianni has dated other women, but I doubt if she wants to hear about them.''

"You're right," Sophia said with compunction. "Gianni would be furious with us, and I wouldn't blame him.''

"You don't have to worry about me," Jillian assured them. "I just work for Gianni. We aren't romantically involved.

Antonia made a wry face. "After the way we've been talking about him, you probably wouldn't want to be.''

"We didn't mean to gossip," Sophia said. "We're all terribly fond of Gianni. We'd love to see him in a caring relationship. He really needs someone. Everybody does.''

"Women like to think that, but Gianni is the most self-sufficient man I ever met," Jillian said.

"Did I hear my name mentioned?" He had strolled over to them, unnoticed by the cluster of women.

They smiled nervously and all started to talk at once.

"I thought you men were never going to join us."

"What do you find to talk about that's so fascinating?"

"Would anyone like more coffee?" Sophia asked.

Gianni gave them a puzzled look and glanced at Jillian for enlightenment. But she just grinned mischievously.

The party broke up soon after that. On the way back to his villa, Gianni asked Jillian what had gone on in the drawing room.

"We were talking about the ball," she said. "They wanted to know what you planned to wear."

"That's scarcely a subject that would panic them if I overheard. Now tell me what you were really talking about."

"I was just listening," Jillian answered demurely.

They had reached his villa and Gianni's attention was diverted. After docking the boat, he snaked a mooring rope around one of the red-and-white-striped poles and helped Jillian onto the pier.

She thought he'd forgotten about their conversation, but when they went inside he took her hand and led her into the den. The lamps were still lit, giving the room a cozy feeling.

"All right, now I want to know what they told you about me," he said.

She knew he wouldn't be pleased at having his love life discussed. In spite of his flamboyant lifestyle, Gianni guarded his personal life zealously.

She tried to find some way of satisfying his curiosity without betraying his friends.

"We really *were* talking about the ball. They said the countess wanted the two of you to go as the king and queen of France."

"Sylvie mentioned it," he said without inflection.

Jillian slanted a glance at him and bent the truth a little. "They also said she was going to be your hostess at the ball. I didn't know that."

"You must have misunderstood. When I planned this party I decided not to ask a date because I'll need to give all of my attention to my guests." He gazed at her consideringly. "I can't be everywhere, though, and little things are bound to come up where I can use a bit of help. Would you mind pitching in?"

"I'd be happy to do anything I can. You don't have to ask. It's part of my job."

"I didn't ask you to the ball as an employee. I want you to enjoy yourself. I just thought you might keep an eye on things while you're circulating around. Like, see that nobody is standing in a corner being ignored."

"That will most likely happen to me. I don't know these people. Not that I'll mind if nobody talks to me," Jillian added hastily. "It will be a treat just to be at the party of the year."

"I'm sure you won't be ignored. Everybody at Sophia's tonight thought you were charming."

"Most likely they were being polite. They're very nice people."

"It's easy to be nice to you."

She could feel the atmosphere between them change. They were facing each other and the warmth of the lamp light was reflected in Gianni's husky voice.

"Well, I, uh, it's getting late," she said. "I guess we'd better go to bed." Her cheeks turned pink as she added hurriedly, "I didn't mean—"

He took her hand and brought it to his lips. "Don't worry, my dear. I'd be very honored if I thought that was an invitation, but I know it isn't."

Jillian wished she could think of something sophisticated to say, something as lightly amused as his remark. But she decided not to push her luck. The sexual attraction between them was quiveringly apparent. It wouldn't take much to ignite the fuse.

Ignoring his comment she turned away and said, "Thanks for a lovely evening. I'll see you in the morning."

Jillian lay awake in the darkness, trying to put Gianni out of her mind. She'd been busy since early morning, and tomorrow was another work day. She couldn't afford to lie here fantasizing about her employer—because that was all Gianni would ever be to her.

But it was difficult to forget that charged moment when desire had spun a silken web, drawing them closer together. If she'd indicated the slightest willingness he would have taken her in his arms and she would finally have felt that firm mouth moving over hers, bringing the promise of ecstasy.

Would he have made love to her there on the carpet, with the lamplight gilding their naked, twisting bodies? Jillian sat up in bed and threw aside the covers. This had to stop! Gianni was a handsome, exciting man, but she didn't indulge in meaningless affairs, and that's all this would be. He wasn't able to commit to any woman, and she couldn't have a relationship unless more than sex was involved.

She got out of bed and went to the door, deciding to go downstairs to the den for something to read. Bookcases were built into the wall on both sides of the fireplace. She had to get some sleep, and a good book was the only way she would get her mind off Gianni.

Jillian hadn't bothered to put on a robe. Gianni would have gone to bed by now and the servants were all asleep. She walked down the carpeted stairs barefoot, guided by moonlight coming through various windows.

The den was dark because the lamps had been turned off and heavy draperies covered the windows. Jillian remembered that a lamp was located next to a couch, but she could only make out vague shapes in the darkness.

As she was moving toward where the couch should be, she suddenly tripped over an object on the carpet and lost her balance. She reached out for something to grab onto, then let out a strangled little scream as two arms closed around her and drew her against a hard body.

"Don't be frightened." Gianni's deep voice was soothing. "You just tripped over my foot."

Her eyes were adjusting to the darkness and she could see that he had been sitting there silently in a wing chair.

"What are you doing here?" she exclaimed. "I thought you'd gone to bed long ago."

"I could ask you the same question," he said in an abstracted voice.

Jillian was very conscious of his lips just inches from her cheek. She was sprawled across his lap, cradled in his arms against his taut body. She knew she should get up. Her thin chiffon nightie was hiked up to her thighs and twisted around her torso. She was practically nude in his arms, something Gianni was discovering as he caressed her back.

She caught her breath when his arms tightened around her and his lips slid down her cheek to the corner of her mouth. "I couldn't sleep," she whispered.

"I couldn't, either." Their breath mingled as his mouth was poised over her parted lips. "What do you think we should do about it?"

Jillian was drowning in his magnetism. His sensuous mouth and seductive hands were arousing her almost unbearably. She wanted to fling her arms around his neck and pull his head down, to feel his mouth take total possession of hers.

"You're so exquisite," he murmured. "I want to

make love to you all night long. Would you like that, my darling?''

How could she say no? Jillian closed her eyes and made a tiny sound of happiness as Gianni's deep kiss fed her rising passion. She quivered and pressed closer to him when his hand caressed her bare thigh. Gianni was everything she'd been looking for in a man, and not only physically. She'd fallen madly, hopelessly in love with him. It was useless to pretend any longer.

He lifted his head to look at her with blazing eyes. ''My beautiful angel, you're going to be mine, aren't you? I'm going to possess you completely!''

Jillian stirred uneasily as his words penetrated her passion-fogged brain. They were ominously prophetic. Gianni wouldn't be affected emotionally if they made love, but she would be. He would indeed possess her, body and soul. And that mustn't be allowed to happen. The hot tide inside her receded as she drew away and tried to straighten her gown.

''Jillian?'' He lifted her chin and gazed at the long lashes fanning her hot cheeks. ''Is something wrong?''

She slid off his lap and stood, wrapping her arms around her trembling body. ''I don't think this is a good idea.'' When he didn't answer, she slanted a wary look at him.

Gianni was staring at her with an unreadable expression. Then he rose from the chair and smiled wryly. ''I don't agree with you, but no means no.''

''I'm sorry,'' she whispered.

''I am, too.'' He reached out and smoothed her tumbled hair. ''I think we would have been quite wonderful together, but only if you felt the same way.''

Jillian didn't trust herself to answer. It was difficult enough to turn her back on something she wanted so much. Gianni must never know just *how* much! Without another word she turned and ran out of the room.

Gianni felt the ache in his loins intensify as he watched her graceful, nearly nude body disappear out the door. He couldn't remember ever wanting a woman this badly. Which was a good reason for not making love to her. He had a feeling that Jillian wouldn't be just a pleasant memory afterward. She was the kind of woman who became as necessary to a man as breathing.

''Thank the Lord one of us showed some common sense,'' he muttered.

Chapter Seven

Jillian dreaded having to face Gianni the next day. What could she say to him? But her worries were groundless. He put her at ease by teasing her about what had happened, as he had once before. Although, that other incident was child's play compared to this one!

"Did you get any sleep last night?" he asked. "I had to take a long, cold shower."

"Sorry about that." She tried to match his flip tone. "I guess I learned not to walk around in the middle of the night in my nightie."

"Not unless you'd consider switching to one of those flannel granny gowns."

She was relieved when the phone rang. Gianni

waited to hear if the call was for him. When it wasn't, he slid his hip off the edge of her desk and started for the door.

Jillian had a mixed bag kind of day. On the plus side, she received a phone call from a famous Italian movie actor. Her excitement at talking to such a superstar was tempered by his request for three more deluxe rooms at the exclusive hotel where she'd booked him a suite. He was bringing a whole entourage—who, incidentally, weren't on the guest list.

Jillian could manage to squeeze in his extra guests, but getting them the kind of accommodations the actor expected was another matter. She had already reserved all the best rooms at the top hotels. She spent the rest of the morning coaxing, flattering and pleading with hotel managers.

The afternoon raised more important problems. The head of the security company called to warn her that he'd received a tip about an infamous jewel thief who was expected in Venice at the time of Gianni's party. The security chief wanted authorization to hire more guards, equip them with walkie talkies and station them prominently throughout the palazzo on the night of the ball.

Jillian knew that Gianni didn't want his guests to feel uncomfortable, but on the other hand, they would be even more upset if they lost a fortune in jewelry. She had to discuss the pros and cons with him, but he was gone all afternoon.

Late in the day, when Jillian thought no other

problems could arise, she received a surprise phone call from her sister. They called each other sparingly because overseas calls were so expensive.

"Is anything wrong?" she asked when she heard her sister's voice.

"No, everything is just perfect!" Bettina answered.

"Then why are you calling? Are Mom and Dad okay?"

"Oh, Jill, you're such a worrywart! Aren't you glad to hear from me? I haven't talked to you in ages."

"I'm thrilled to hear from you—as long as everything is okay. How is married life?"

"I heartily recommend it," Bettina said with a bubbly little laugh. "When are *you* going to tie the knot?"

"We're so busy right now with the ball that we haven't had time to think about anything else. Guess who I talked to on the phone today? Marcello Darmatti! And guess what? He sounds just as sexy in real life."

"What did you talk about? I would have freaked out and not known what to say to him."

"We didn't talk long, but he was very nice."

"That's so cool! You're really hobnobbing with the rich and famous. Who would have thought a vacation in Venice would change your entire life?"

"Your life must be exciting, too. What are you and David doing with yourselves this summer?—

besides making love and generally enjoying married bliss.''

"Well, that's why I called you. David and I talked it over and we decided to use our wedding money for a honeymoon. It will be difficult to get away once we go back to college in the fall. If we don't take it now, we'll have to postpone it indefinitely.''

"That would be a shame. Everybody deserves a honeymoon. And you're right. If you try to find time during the school year, one or the other of you will have exams or a paper to write. You definitely should do it now.''

"I'm so glad you agree because we want to come to Venice.''

Jillian was speechless for a moment. This just wasn't her day!

"The air fare will eat up most of our money,'' Bettina continued. "So the only way we can swing it is if we stay at Gianni's. Will that be okay?''

"No!'' Jillian modified her tone hastily. "I mean, you don't even know each other. I can't ask him to take in two complete strangers.''

"That's a funny way of putting it. Maybe we've never met, but we're going to be family. David and I aren't some couple you struck up a conversation with at a coffee house. Gianni is going to be our brother-in-law.''

"But he isn't yet. I don't think it's wise to start off by asking for favors.''

"What's going on, Jill?'' Bettina asked slowly.

"Are you ashamed of your family? Is that why you don't want Gianni to meet us?"

"Of course not! How could you even think such a thing?"

"What other explanation is there? I thought you'd be as thrilled as I was. We haven't seen each other for ages."

"I know, and I miss you terribly."

"But you don't want us to come to Venice," Bettina said in a flat tone.

"That's not so. I do want you to come. I just don't think it's a good idea for you to stay with Gianni."

"Why not? You said he has this huge palazzo with a bunch of bedrooms and a whole staff of servants to take care of the place. It isn't like we'd be crowding him. If the house is that big he'd hardly even know we were there."

Jillian searched wildly for a valid objection. "The fact that he has room is beside the point. It would be different if Gianni and I were married. Then it would be my house, too, and of course you'd be welcome."

"That's just plain silly! You're engaged, aren't you?"

"Well, I, uh…yes, but that's not the same as being married. Something could happen," Jillian said vaguely. "You never know."

"Are you telling me the engagement is off? Is that why you're trying to discourage us from coming?"

"I didn't say it was off. I just meant, sometimes couples decide they're not right for each other."

"If you and Gianni broke up, why didn't you come home? What are you still doing there?"

"You're twisting my words around," Jillian insisted. "I didn't say the engagement was off, I merely said I didn't want to be in Gianni's debt in case something *did* happen."

Bettina was scarcely listening. "I know it's been rough for you since David and I announced our engagement. Everybody pestering you about when *you* were going to get married. People can be so insensitive. But you can't just invent a glamorous fiancé in some far-away place and then expect everybody to believe you changed your mind about marrying him. People will laugh at you behind your back."

Jillian suppressed a groan. Bettina was right, although in all fairness, she hadn't made up the entire story. One thing had just led to another. Yet how could she tell her sister the truth? Bettina would tell David, and he would tell someone, warning that person not to tell anyone else. It wouldn't take very long for the story to get around. She couldn't face the ridicule.

Taking a deep breath, Jillian said, "I didn't dream up Gianni or his palazzo on the Grand Canal. They're both everything I said they were. He's sexy and gorgeous and rich—but more than that, I'm crazy about him."

"Okay, if all of that is true then there's something else you're not telling me. What is it, Jill? You know

you can tell me anything. We used to be so close,''
Bettina said plaintively.

"We still are." Jillian felt terrible. "Maybe I am
being foolish. Gianni is a very generous man. I'll
talk to him. And if for any reason he isn't enthusiastic about the idea, then I'll get you and David a
room at my hotel. Start packing. You're going to
spend your honeymoon in Venice, and we're going
to have a fantastic time.''

"I couldn't let you pay for our hotel," Bettina
protested.

"Why not? I'm making a great salary and I can't
think of any way I'd rather spend it.''

"Well…talk to Gianni and then we'll discuss it.''

"There's nothing to discuss, you're coming! You
can do me a favor, too. If you have room in your
suitcase I'd like you to bring me a few things from
home.''

They talked about what kind of clothes Bettina
should bring, and Jillian mentioned some of the
places she wanted to take them. They were so excited about seeing each other again that they both
talked at once.

Finally Jillian said, "We'd better hang up. This
is costing you a fortune.''

"It's worth it. I never dreamed I'd be honey-
mooning in Venice! I'll just die if anything happens
and we can't come!''

"I never dreamed I'd be joining you on your honeymoon," Jillian laughed. "And don't worry, only
good things are going to happen.''

Her smile faded after she'd hung up. How was she going to keep her sister from finding out the truth about her relationship with Gianni? He wouldn't mind having her family stay here, but she could scarcely ask him to pretend to be her fiancé.

Maybe the best idea would be for the newlyweds to stay at her hotel, as she suggested. But she couldn't keep them away from Gianni entirely. They would expect to see his villa, even if they weren't invited to stay. And of course they'd expect to meet Gianni. Jillian rested her head in her hands. How was she ever going to get herself out of this latest mess?

"More problems?" Gianni was standing in the doorway.

Her head popped up and she tried to look unconcerned. "No...I mean, yes, a couple. If you have a minute I'd like to talk to you about a few things that came up today."

"Anything serious? You look a little overwhelmed."

"One of them could be serious. It involves security. I'll tell you what the chief told me, and let you decide."

"All right. Come up to my room in fifteen minutes. I've been playing tennis, and I want to take a quick shower and change clothes."

Maybe she wouldn't mention her own dilemma tonight, Jillian thought, after he left. Gianni had expected the necessary guards to mingle unobtrusively with the guests, not be an obvious presence with walkie talkies. He was also apt to be annoyed that the Italian movie star was bringing so many uninvited guests. Why upset him further?

When Jillian showed up at Gianni's suite a short time later, he had showered and was toweling his hair dry. He had on a pair of slacks, but no shoes or shirt. She almost forgot what she wanted to talk to him about. How could she concentrate on anything but his bare chest and the way it tapered in a triangle down to his flat stomach and lean hips?

Making a conscious effort to look only at his face, she said, "I should have given you more time. Do you want me to come back?"

"No, I can finish getting dressed while we talk. Sit down and tell me what's so important that I have to decide." He gestured toward the sitting room at the opposite end of the huge bedroom.

Jillian took a seat on the down-filled couch by the fireplace. While Gianni shrugged into a cream-colored silk shirt, she told him about the problems they faced with security.

As she expected, he was less than happy about the proposed change in plans. He paced the floor as they discussed alternatives, then came to sit next to her on the couch.

Gianni took the news of the uninvited guests more philosophically. "I suppose we can squeeze in a few more people, although we must be reaching the saturation point."

"Not to mention the fact that we're driving the

caterer crazy. I keep upping the count every other day.''

''Adding up the bill will alleviate his pain,'' Gianni observed cynically.

''It's going to equal the gross national product of a small country.''

''Don't sound so disapproving. Look at what I'm doing for the economy, all the goods and services I'm generating,'' he teased.

He was joking, but it was true. Many segments of the city were benefiting from Gianni's party. She hadn't meant to sound disapproving, but Jillian couldn't help feeling that Gianni needed more than social events to occupy his mind. He was too bright to lead the life of a dilettante.

She stared at him curiously. ''Are you really friendly with all these people?''

''More or less. We exchange parties and see each other at resorts and charity benefits.''

''You certainly lead a busy social life. It's a good thing you don't have to juggle a job, too.''

He looked at her without expression. ''This isn't the first time you've accused me of being a grasshopper in a world of ants.''

''I wasn't accusing you of anything. Why should you work when you don't have to?''

''Just because I don't work set hours for a predetermined salary doesn't mean I'm a hedonist, interested only in my own pleasure.'' For the first time, he seemed genuinely annoyed at her.

Jillian regretted her implied criticism. She, of all

people, knew how kind and generous Gianni was.
"I didn't mean to sound judgmental. I'm sorry if it
came out that way."

"It's what you think that matters. For your information, a good part of my week is taken up with
my family's foundation. We support various causes,
from medical research to the needs of the elderly. I
read every one of the dozens of reports submitted to
me, so I can make informed decisions on where the
funding is most needed."

"I didn't realize that," she murmured.

"I don't advertise the fact. Or call attention to my
position as a trustee on various boards, like the
Wildlife Rescue Mission, and the Worldwide Children's Fund. I'll be attending their conference in
Paris soon after the ball."

"People should know things like that! Then they
wouldn't think all you do is go to parties and give
them. That's what the gossip columns imply."

"It doesn't usually bother me." He gave her a
slightly baffled look. "I don't know why I feel the
need to justify myself to you."

"You *don't* need to! I'm ashamed of myself for
what I said."

He shrugged. "Why? if that's what you think…"

"But I don't! I was just puzzled that you weren't
doing anything meaningful when you're so intelligent and vital."

Gianni smiled sardonically. "You don't have to
overdo it."

"I'm being sincere. I've seen what a caring per-

son you are. Look what you did for me, a total
stranger. I don't know what I would have done without you.''

''You helped me out, too, so consider us even.
You've handled a difficult job very competently.''

''Cross your fingers! I just hope everything goes
off without a hitch,'' she said.

''It will, and if there are some glitches it won't
be the end of the world. It's only a party. Are there
any other problems you need to discuss with me?
Now is the time to get them all out of the way.''

Jillian hesitated. She really should mention that
Bettina and David were coming. Gianni had to
know, since she couldn't keep her relatives a secret
for their entire visit. Maybe now wasn't the best
time to tell him, though. Not right after she'd irri-
tated him by questioning his lifestyle, or at least
seeming to.

Summoning a smile, she said, ''No. Those were
the only problems.''

''Are you sure? You have a very expressive face.
It's not conducive to lying,'' he teased.

She opened her eyes wide and gazed at him in-
nocently. ''What would I have to lie about?''

''That's what I'd like to know. You might as well
tell me. I'll find out anyway.''

''Not right away,'' she muttered.

''So you *are* keeping something from me.''

''Nothing important, and it doesn't concern you
anyway.'' She paused before taking the plunge.
''My sister called a little while ago. She and her

husband are planning to spend their honeymoon in Venice.''

''That's great news! I know how much you've missed your family.'' Gianni gave her a quizzical look. ''You should be happy that they're coming.''

''I am. It's just that this isn't the greatest time they could have picked, with the ball so imminent, I mean.''

''It's a perfect time. They'll be here for the party. It should be something a little different for them. I'll look forward to meeting your sister.''

''Yes, well, they'll probably be busy every minute sightseeing. They've never been to Venice before. I know they'll be thrilled to come to the ball, though.''

Jillian knew a court order couldn't keep Bettina and David away once her sister found out they were invited. But Gianni would be so busy that night that they wouldn't have time to say more than a few words to each other. It would be nerve-racking, but things might still work out.

''I like showing off my city,'' Gianni said. ''We'll take them to places that tourists don't know about.''

''Well, see, that's the problem. Things are speeding up now and I can't take a lot of time off. That's why I said this isn't the best time.''

''You're being overly conscientious. All the major arrangements have been finalized. You'll have plenty of time to spend with your sister. And when you're busy, I'll show them around.''

"No!" Jillian tried to fight down her rising panic. "I couldn't ask you to do that, not after I just discovered all the important things you're involved in. Besides, they're my responsibility."

Something occurred to Gianni. "Where are they planning to stay?"

"I'll get them a room at my hotel."

"That's ridiculous when I have all these empty bedrooms. They can stay with me. You can move in, too. It will save you time and you'll get to see more of them."

She could tell he wasn't going to take no for an answer. Her deception was unraveling like a piece of knitting.

"There's something you should know." Jillian realized she couldn't put it off any longer. "Remember when you advised me to call my parents and tell them that Rinaldo and I had decided to postpone our wedding until we knew each other better? I told them I'd gotten a job so I could stay here, but my Dad was skeptical. He knew I'd need a work permit."

Gianni nodded. "So you told him you were working temporarily for a friend of Rinaldo's."

"That's what I *should* have told them. But I got rattled. I told you I have trouble lying. What I really said was that I was working for my fiancé."

"Rinaldo?" Gianni asked disapprovingly.

"No, *you.*"

"I don't understand."

"I don't blame you." She sighed. "I didn't want

to mention you because I thought it would just complicate matters. My parents would have asked a million questions—where we met, why you'd offer a job to a total stranger. They would have been sure you had an ulterior motive and they would have worried themselves sick.''

''I guess I can understand that, but I'd have been happy to talk to them and explain things.''

''What could you say? That you came to my rescue after I called off the wedding because the groom's girlfriend brought their baby to the church? That's what I was trying to prevent my parents from finding out.''

''Yes, I see the problem.''

''I happened to mention your name accidentally, and somehow my parents got the idea that you're my fiancé.'' Jillian held her breath, waiting for the explosion.

Gianni was frowning, as she had expected, but only because he was trying to sort it all out. ''How could they think that when you'd already told them his name was Rinaldo?''

''I changed his name, but that's another story.''

Gianni looked amused. ''I can't wait to hear it.''

''You're better off not knowing,'' she muttered.

''All right, I'm Rinaldo, only I suddenly became Gianni. But you and I are engaged and you work for me. Is that part right?''

''Yes.''

''So, what's the problem? Nothing has changed. When you decide you want to go home you'll stick to your original story. That after really getting to know Rinaldo—or whatever his name is—you found out he wasn't right for you.''

"You're forgetting about Bettina and David. They know everything about you from my letters. I described your villa down to the last detail. In fact, I overdid it. Bettina couldn't understand why I didn't want to ask you to let them stay here.''

"I'm not surprised. You must have known I'd be delighted to have them.''

"That would be a disaster! After they saw us together they'd know I made up the whole thing.''

"If that's all that's bothering you, you're getting upset over nothing. I can manage to look adoring if you can.'' He grinned.

"You're not angry?'' she asked uncertainly.

"On the contrary, I'm flattered.''

Jillian wasn't reassured by the mischief in his eyes. Gianni meant well, but he would give the game away by camping it up. Her shoulders slumped dejectedly. "It will never work. What on earth am I going to do?''

Gianni took both of her hands in his. "You're going to call your sister and tell her I'd be delighted to have her and her husband stay here. And then I'll take the phone and tell her how much I'm looking forward to meeting them.''

When she looked at him doubtfully, he picked up the telephone from an end table and handed it to her.

Bettina sounded wary when she heard her sister's

voice. "Please don't tell me we can't come for some reason."

"No, everything is all arranged. You'll be staying at Gianni's."

"You asked him!"

"Actually he was the one who suggested it."

"I knew he would! I couldn't understand why you didn't want to ask him."

"Yes, well, you're all set."

"You don't sound very enthusiastic. Is something wrong that you're not telling me, Jill? Did you and Gianni argue? I hope it wasn't over David and me!"

"No, of course not. I mean, we didn't argue. Everything is fine between us."

Gianni looked at her questioningly. "Is there a problem?"

She put her hand over the mouthpiece. "She can tell there's something funny going on. I told you we'd never get away with it."

He took the phone out of her hand. "Bettina? This is Gianni. Jillian and I are so pleased that you're coming for a visit. She's told me so much about her family, and now I'll finally get to meet you."

"I'm dying to meet you, too. If even half the things Jill wrote about you are true, you must be a combination of Superman and Pierce Brosnan." Bettina laughed breathlessly.

"People in love are entitled to exaggerate."

"She's certainly mad about you. Do you really

have a profile that could grace a Roman coin? I've never known Jill to be that poetic.''

''Don't expect too much. Your sister is the beauty in this family.''

''What is she telling you?'' Jillian asked in alarm.

''We're just getting acquainted,'' he answered with a reassuring smile.

''You have to be as special as she says,'' Bettina said. ''Jill has never raved this way about any other man.''

''I realize how lucky I am.''

Jillian couldn't stand the suspense any longer. ''Let me talk to her.'' She took the phone out of his hand. ''Bettina? I'm sorry to cut this short, but Gianni and I have to go out. Call me when you know what flight you'll be on.''

''I will. Oh, Jill, he sounds divine!''

''Yes, he is pretty wonderful.'' She gave Gianni a weak smile.

''I'm so glad I was just imagining things—about you two having problems, I mean. He's obviously wild about you, too. I'm so excited! The four of us are going to have such fun.''

After she'd hung up, Gianni said, ''There, that wasn't so bad, was it?''

''I guess not. At least Bettina isn't suspicious anymore. Thanks to you, I dodged the bullet one more time.''

''Not completely.'' He grinned impishly. ''You evidently let your imagination run wild in your letters to her. If I'm as great as you told her, she'll want to know all the intimate details.''

''I'll just say there is nothing to tell.''

''You're going to pretend we don't make love? You're not very knowledgeable about Italian men— or men in general, for that matter.'' His expression changed as he said softly, ''If you were promised to me, I'd want to hold you in my arms all night long.''

Her heartbeat quickened as she imagined their nude bodies twined together. Moistening her dry lips, she tried to defuse the dangerous situation by treating it as a joke.

''Maybe it *will* work after all. You have that throaty voice and smoldering gaze down pat. I only hope I can do half as well.''

''Perhaps we should practice our act—especially the part where we kiss,'' he said with a little smile.

''We can be convincing without that.''

''People in love kiss.''

He lifted her chin and lowered his face until their lips were only a whisper apart. Jillian reached out to brace her hands against his chest, but somehow they slid up to his shoulders, and then tangled in his thick hair.

Gianni's mouth closed over hers for a kiss that was scorching in intensity. As he probed the warm recess of her mouth, his arms wrapped her tightly against his taut frame.

She uttered a tiny cry of delight and arched her body into his. This was what she'd dreamed about, ever since that night in the den when he'd held her like this. She had let her head overrule her heart then, but no more. Love wasn't cautious. If this was all Gianni had to give her, she would take it.

He drew back slightly to look into her eyes. ''Sweet, beautiful Jillian, you must know how much I want to make love to you. But I don't want you to do anything you'll be sorry for.''

Giving him an enchanting smile, she said, ''I'll be a lot sorrier if I don't.''

Chapter Eight

Gianni's mouth closed over Jillian's for a kiss that made liquid fire leap through her veins. His sensuous tongue explored the warm, wet recess of her mouth with symbolic thrusts that quickened her breathing.

Her hands traced the width of his broad shoulders restlessly before digging into the lithe muscles in his back. She caressed his throat, then tangled her fingers in his thick hair, like a blind person discovering treasure.

"My lovely, passionate beauty," Gianni said hoarsely, gazing at her with blazing eyes. "I've wanted you from the first moment I saw you."

"Don't tell me. Show me how much."

"I intend to—all night long."

He lifted her in his arms and carried her over to the bed. Standing her on her feet, he grasped the hem of her sweater and pulled it over her head. His movements seemed tantalizingly deliberate as he unclasped her bra and slowly removed it.

Her skin was exquisitely sensitized by his avid gaze. She quivered with anticipation. When his long fingers stroked her breasts she moaned softly and swayed toward him.

"You're so responsive, *cara mia*," he said in a thickened voice. "I love watching your expressive face when I bring you pleasure. You have such a beautiful body. I'm going to know every inch of it."

She felt the same urgent need to touch him. Unbuttoning his shirt, she lowered her head to slide her lips across his bare chest. Gianni drew in his breath sharply, and when she slid her hands inside the waistband of his slacks and dug her fingers into his rigid buttocks he groaned with pleasure.

Jillian had never felt such need. Her inhibitions vanished as she slid his zipper down and pushed his slacks and briefs over his hips. His nude body was awesome. She ran her palms over his flat stomach, his muscular thighs. But when she stoked him intimately, Gianni cried out and grabbed her hands.

"I want it to be good for you, *cara,* but I'm only human. You don't know what you're doing to me," he said, breathing hard.

She smiled enchantingly. "It's pretty evident."

"You're *trying* to make me lose control, aren't you?"

"Yes!" She felt wild and free. "I want you to need me so much that you couldn't stop now if you tried."

"You've got your wish." He swiftly removed her skirt and the brief panties that were her only other garment. "You're as necessary to me as breathing. I need to be part of you."

His hands gripped her hips and pulled them to his. The scorching heat they were both generating made Jillian liquid inside. Anticipation had built to a fever pitch and neither could wait any longer.

Gianni lifted her slightly and plunged deeply inside her. She wrapped her legs around his waist and her arms around his neck. His mouth reached for hers and they rocketed into a world of pure sensation. They were joined in every way possible, sharing equally in the passion that passed from his body to hers and back again.

The pounding waves mounted higher and higher, thundering through them, struggling to a distant shore. Then a final wave washed away the frenzied urgency and they floated peacefully, rocked rather than buffeted.

They clung together for long minutes before he carried her over to the bed and settled her gently among the pillows without releasing her. Their damp bodies were relaxed and their breathing slowly returned to normal. They were utterly fulfilled, but neither wanted to be separated from the other.

Gianni finally stirred. "What can I say? You're incredible."

She smiled without opening her eyes. "You're pretty awesome yourself."

"I can't believe all the fire you've been hiding under that prim exterior," he teased.

She couldn't either. Falling in love with Gianni had changed her. She knew now what she wanted, what she'd been looking for without knowing what it was. A man who had all the qualities she admired, someone she could share the rest of her life with.

But how did *he* feel? He hadn't said he loved her, not even at the height of their passion. It had been so swift, though. They hadn't had time for words, only emotions. But surely his actions spoke for him. Gianni had been as swept away as she. Jillian gazed at him through her lashes, looking for reassurance.

He misinterpreted her veiled gaze. Kissing her eyelids, he said, "Don't be shy with me, darling. I was only teasing you."

"Do you like women to take the initiative? Some men might feel their masculinity was being usurped."

"I have no problems in that department. Feel free to make advances anytime you like." He grinned.

"You've got a deal, but I'll use discretion. Harry's Bar might disapprove."

"If they're that unenlightened, we won't go there." He smoothed the long hair off her forehead and kissed her sweetly. "I hope I made you as happy as you made me."

"You were wonderful," she said softly, stroking his cheek.

"I wasn't looking for compliments, just reassurance that it was even half the experience for you that it was for me."

He really cared, she thought, her heart swelling with joy. She just had to be patient. Gianni was wary of commitment, but that would change if she didn't crowd him.

"Let me put it this way," she said. "I won't have any trouble convincing Bettina that you're the greatest."

"It was a pleasure to solve all your problems."

"I just hope I haven't created any problems for *you*," she said artlessly.

"I can't think what they would be." Gianni trailed his fingers erotically along her inner thigh. "I have remarkable stamina. I can make love to you as often as you'll let me."

"I was thinking about Bettina and David's visit. If we should run into any of your friends while we're taking them around, they're very apt to mention our supposed engagement."

Gianni's wandering hand stilled and he drew away slightly. "I hadn't thought of that."

"We'd better decide what to say in case it comes up."

"What do you suggest?"

Something inside of her died. It felt like hope. If Gianni wanted her to be a permanent part of his life he wouldn't worry that their relationship might be misunderstood. What made her think the magic they just shared would make any difference?

"Don't worry," she said, trying to mask her feelings. "I'll make up some reason why we're keeping our engagement a secret."

After a glance at her expressive face, Gianni said, "It isn't that important. Let's not complicate things."

"You're doing me a big favor. I don't want you to have to pay for it."

He gathered her back into his arms. "You did me a much bigger favor. I've never known anyone as sweet and generous as you."

The ice around Jillian's heart thawed a little. "That's a nice compliment, considering all the women you've known."

"I don't remember any of them." His teeth nipped gently at her lower lip as his fingers trailed down her back to trace sensuous patterns across her bottom. "You're the only one who is important to me."

She wanted desperately to believe that, but it would be humiliating to appear needy. Keeping the urgency out of her voice, she said, "We *are* good together."

"That's the understatement of the year!"

He scissored one leg around both of hers and cupped her bottom in both hands. Their hips were joined so closely that she was aware of his arousal. The glowing embers in her midsection ignited, heating her body until it was like pliant wax, molding itself to his.

Time was suspended, and the realities of everyday life. They were lost in each other, all their needs centered in this moment. Caressing each other erotically, they murmured suggestive words between kisses.

Anticipation built as they teased and tantalized, drawing out the pleasure that lay ahead. Jillian never knew she was capable of such abandonment, but Gianni delighted in urging her to push the limits.

"Tell me how you feel when I do this." His wet tongue circled her sensitive nipple. "Or this." He stroked the quiveringly receptive area at the juncture of her thighs.

"No, wait!" she begged, feeling the hot tide he'd set in motion begin to swell. Soon nothing could stop it. "Make love to me now!"

"Not yet. This is just for you. I want to bring you the fulfillment you deserve, and watch you enjoy it."

When his fingers slipped inside of her, Jillian arched her body, pressing against his hand. He skillfully fed her passion until her limbs were taut with tension and she was breathing rapidly. Release came suddenly in a series of spasms that built in intensity, filling her with delight.

Gianni's eyes glittered as he watched the rapture he'd brought about. "Yes, my darling. This is what I wanted for you."

When she held out her arms to him, he plunged

inside of her. His hard driving strength fed the flickering flames until they burst into a roaring blaze again, and she shared his passion joyously.

They were completely spent afterward, content to lie quietly in each other's arms.

It was much later that Gianni finally stirred and kissed her closed eyelids. "Are you hungry?" he asked.

She opened her eyes and laughed. "That's the last thing I expected you to say."

"I was only thinking of you. We used up a lot of energy."

"I have heard that sex burns up quite a few calories," she joked.

"We made love," he corrected her. "That's an entirely different thing."

She stroked his hair tenderly. "You always know how to make people feel good."

"I'm not interested in 'people,' just you." He kissed the tip of her nose, then rolled off the bed. "I'm going to order dinner. Any requests?"

"No, whatever you like." Jillian reached for her discarded clothes. "I'll go get dressed."

"Why don't I give you a robe instead?" He grinned wickedly. "It seems like a waste of time to get dressed, since we'll be going back to bed afterward."

"Stop trying to impress me."

"That wasn't a boast, it was a promise." He came over to frame her face in his palms. "I want to hold you in my arms all night, and wake up to find you there in the morning.''

''I can't stay with you all night, Gianni.''

''You don't imagine I'm going to let you go back to the hotel?''

''No, but I'll sleep in the room I used before. The servants don't need to know about us.''

''What we do doesn't concern anyone—and certainly not the servants. Besides, we're engaged, aren't we?''

''The only ones we want to think that are Bettina and David.'' Jillian was hurt by his flippant tone, as though he couldn't imagine their engagement being anything but a big joke. ''I'm going to my room to take a shower.''

He looked at her with a slight frown. ''Is something wrong?''

''No, I'm just a little tired.'' She mustered a smile. ''It's been a busy day. Maybe I'll just skip dinner.''

''As you wish. Why don't you take a relaxing bubble bath instead of a shower, and then see how you feel?''

''Maybe I'll do that. But I know you must be hungry, so go ahead and eat without me.''

The warm bath relaxed Jillian and she could think more clearly away from Gianni's charismatic presence. Was she refusing to face the truth, that he would never be ready to make a commitment? Probably. So, did that mean tonight had been a mistake?

When she remembered his tenderness, as well as his passion and genuine caring, she knew it hadn't been. If this was all she would ever have, what she'd experienced with him tonight was still worth any pain that would come when their affair was over.

The only mistake would be letting him know that she was in love with him. Gianni was such a decent person. He would feel guilty, and miserable about hurting her. But if he thought she felt as he did, they could have a wonderful, exciting interlude together. And when it was over...well, they'd both have happy memories. Jillian smiled wryly. His would just be a little happier than hers, that's all.

After she had gotten out of the tub and dried herself, she went into the bedroom, wrapped in a towel and with her hair piled on top of her head. She stopped abruptly at the sight of Gianni.

"As usual, you forgot to take a robe in there with you." He was holding his silk robe over his arm.

"I'm surprised you didn't come barging right into the bathroom with it," she teased.

"I never barge, although I must admit I blunder sometimes." He stripped off her towel and gazed at her affectionately. "Do you know how adorable you look with those flushed cheeks and your hair tied up with that pink ribbon?" He helped her into the robe and then took her in his arms.

Over his shoulder she noticed that a tilt top table had been spread with a cloth. It was set for two and covered with silver domed serving dishes.

"Didn't you have dinner yet?" she asked.

''No, I waited for you. But don't worry. I had it brought to my quarters. I carried everything in here myself. And if it will make you happy, I'll take it all back into my room before we go to bed.''

''We?''

''You and me—that's we. If you won't share my bed, I'll share yours.''

''You're crazy, do you know that?'' she said fondly.

''Crazy about you.'' After a brief but satisfying kiss, he pulled out a chair for her at the table.

The days that followed were a pure delight. The masked ball was not much more than two weeks away, so Jillian was busy with last-minute details. But the nights belonged solely to them.

They went out to dinner at romantic little restaurants with a candle flickering in the middle of the table, reflecting the glow they both felt. Then sometimes they would take a long walk along the Grand Canal where gondoliers serenaded starry-eyed tourists and their songs drifted softly in the breeze.

Later they would come home and walk hand in hand up the grand staircase of Gianni's villa, exchanging a glance of sweet anticipation. It was a magical interlude.

If only this could last for a lifetime, Jillian thought wistfully. The improbability of that ever happening made her sad, so she tried not to think of anything past this moment.

Then the day of Bettina's and David's visit arrived and their private idyll was over. They took Gianni's boat to the wharf near the airport, and were waiting when the young couple got off the plane.

Bettina spotted them and waved wildly, grabbing her husband's arm and pointing.

Gianni chuckled indulgently. "They look like your American Ken and Barbie dolls."

Both of the young people were blond, with gleaming white smiles and trim bodies.

Bettina sprinted the last few yards and threw her arms around her sister, exclaiming, "I can't believe we're really here! Are you as excited as I am? You couldn't possibly be! Before I forget, Mom and Dad said to be sure and give you their love."

"You haven't changed," Jillian laughed. "Let me say hello to David, and I want you to meet Gianni."

After the introductions had been made, Gianni and David went to claim the luggage and have it brought to the dock.

"He's *gorgeous!*" Bettina said when she and her sister were alone. "I thought you must be exaggerating—nobody could be that handsome."

"He's a wonderful person, too. That's even more important."

"If you say so," Bettina grinned. "I can't wait to see his palace."

"Venetians call their old mansions palazzos, but most of them aren't really palaces, in the strictest sense of the word."

"I can't believe my own sister is going to be a

duchess. What are we supposed to call you after you're married?—besides lucky.''

''I'll settle for that.'' Jillian changed the subject. ''I want to hear all the latest news. Tell me about you and David.'' That should distract her. ''Have you decided where you're going to live when school starts in the fall?''

The trip down the Grand Canal to the heart of Venice was always impressive. The young couple stood in the bow of the boat, their faces filled with excitement as they drank in the exotic atmosphere and stared at the islands that dotted the busy waterway.

As they passed the Piazza San Marco, they exclaimed over their first glimpse of the famous pigeons gathered in front of St. Mark's Basilica. They were charmed by the narrow, winding streets that led away from the square, and impressed by the other ancient churches with domes and clock towers.

Gianni pointed out the more famous hotels, the Gritti Palace, the Danieli and more. When he rounded a bend and cut the motor at his own dock, Bettina couldn't believe this was his villa.

She and David were equally impressed when they went inside, leaving their luggage for the servants to deal with. ''I feel like I'm in a museum and the guards are going to tell me not to touch anything,'' Bettina said.

''When your house has been in the family for generations, you're stuck with a bunch of ancient hand-me-downs. But don't be intimidated. These rooms are meant to be enjoyed,'' Gianni told her, taking Jillian's hand and leading the way up the curving staircase.

He had chosen a large suite for the young couple, at the opposite end of the house from his. The furnishings were elegant. An intricately carved writing desk had a tooled leather top decorated in gold, and the blue-and-cream handwoven rugs were priceless. Filmy curtains were attached to a crown-shaped ornament on the ceiling over the bed. They could be tied back, or left to flow down gracefully to provide an illusion of privacy.

''Wow!'' David exclaimed. ''My marriage is in trouble already. Betts isn't going to be satisfied with a studio apartment after this.''

''Of course I will,'' she said. ''Normal people don't live like this.''

''Do you want to tell your sister how normal I am?'' Gianni asked Jillian with amusement.

''No,'' she answered briefly. ''I'm going down to my office to see if any faxes came in while we were gone.''

''I hope David and I aren't going to inhibit you,'' Bettina said to her sister. ''Jill was always a little prim,'' she remarked to Gianni as the servants brought in their luggage.

''Really? That isn't a word I'd use to describe her.''

''Let's let them get unpacked,'' Jillian said.

''Right.'' He put his arm around her shoulders and walked her to the door. ''Come downstairs when you're settled in and we'll make plans for the evening," he told the other couple.

When they were far enough down the hall to be out of hearing, Jillian said, "I appreciate what you're doing, but you're layering it on a little thick."

"I was being honest. How can I think of you as prim after last night?"

They had made love to the music of the water gently lapping against the pier outside, while beams of silvery moonlight filtered through the shutters and shimmered over their nude bodies. Jillian had been unrestrained in Gianni's arms. She had explored his body almost greedily, caressing him so erotically that he cried out, then turned the tables by making her plead for his embrace.

"A gentleman doesn't remind a lady of her wanton behavior." She tried not to smile, and failed.

"That's not what I'd call it." He took her in his arms and kissed her sweetly. "You were exciting and irresistible. You make our nights together pure magic."

Jillian melted inside. She was so afraid she'd blurt out her love for him that she laughed awkwardly and said, "You still can't stay all night with me while Bettina and David are here."

"Do you really think they'd disapprove?"

"No, but I'd be self-conscious."

"All right." He sighed. "I won't argue about it— as long as I have visiting privileges."

"I'd miss you if you didn't take advantage of them," she said softly.

"That's something you'll never have to worry about."

Jillian was returning to her room after checking for messages in the office, when her sister called to her from down the hall.

"I've been knocking on doors, looking for you. I forgot to ask where Gianni's room was." Bettina came inside and looked around with expectation that turned to surprise. "I thought he'd have a suite like ours, only grander."

"He does. This is the room I use when we come home late, and I don't feel like going back to the hotel. I'll be staying here during your visit."

"You're not living here with Gianni? You must be out of your mind!"

"No, it makes good sense. We decided not to move too fast."

"That sounds like *your* decision, not his."

"It was mutual."

"If you say so. But I can't imagine a virile guy like Gianni agreeing to a setup like that without some serious arm twisting."

"Does he strike you as the kind of man who can be pushed around?"

"No," Bettina admitted. "But if I was engaged to somebody like Gianni, you can bet I wouldn't sleep alone. What a hunk! I'll bet he's a terrific lover, too."

"If you're looking for details, forget it. And that doesn't make me prim—just private."

"When did you get so private? We used to tell each other everything about the men in our lives."

That was before she had this much to tell, Jillian reflected. It was going to be even more difficult than she anticipated, keeping her sister from suspecting anything.

"Would you consider me nosy if I asked why you postponed the wedding?" Bettina asked. "You're obviously crazy about each other."

This was the tricky part. Jillian had to agree that she and Gianni were in love, yet leave herself an out when she eventually announced that they'd decided not to marry.

"There's a lot more to marriage than sex," she began carefully. "You have to be compatible in other ways, too. For one thing, Gianni's background and mine are poles apart. I don't know if I could adapt to his lifestyle."

"Yeah, that would really be tough! Living in the height of luxury, being waited on by a staff of servants. I can see where that might make you miserable."

"I would also be living in a foreign country, away from everything that was familiar to me. Big houses and glamorous parties sound exciting, but what if I didn't fit in?" Her sister didn't need to know she'd already passed that test.

"I guess you might have a few problems, but nothing you couldn't handle. You've always been good with people, and you can come home for visits if you get homesick. It isn't like you'd be strapped for money.''

"Everything *sounds* easy, but I want to be sure. That's why Gianni and I haven't announced our engagement. If we bump into any of his friends while we're out, I'd rather you didn't mention it.'' Jillian hoped it sounded like a casual request.

"You almost got married. Weren't any of his friends invited to the wedding?''

"No, we intended to elope and announce it at a reception afterward.''

"How about his family? You mentioned once that Gianni has a sister.''

"He didn't tell her, either. She's kind of wrapped up in her own problems.''

"I see.'' Bettina didn't sound as if she did.

"It's no big deal if people find out. I'm sure we'll get around to setting a date after the ball is over. I'd just feel more comfortable, and I'm sure Gianni would, too, if everybody didn't pester us with a lot of questions about the big event.''

"Whatever you say.''

Bettina went back to her own room soon after that. David was coming out of the bathroom with a towel wrapped around his trim midsection.

"You gotta check out all the stuff in that bathroom!'' he said. "It's unreal!''

"That's nice,'' she answered vaguely.

"Is anything wrong?'' David looked at her with a slight frown.

"I don't know. I got some very mixed messages from Jill."

"About our being here, you mean? She seemed really glad to see us."

"It isn't that. I'm worried about her and Gianni. Do you know she only stays here occasionally?"

"You're yanking my chain!"

"That's what she told me. But something bothers me even more. She asked me not to tell anybody that they're engaged—his people, I mean."

"Did she say why?"

"Oh sure, but it didn't make a lot of sense. At least, not to me. What do you think is going on? First she's going to get married, then they're going to be engaged for a while instead, now even the engagement sounds iffy."

"Don't jump to conclusions. There could be all kinds of reasons for keeping it a secret."

"Name one."

"I can't think of any off the top of my head, but I can tell when two people are in love. And those two are a walking advertisement."

"They do seem to be mad about each other, but I know my sister. She's a very open person. Her engagement is the last thing she'd want to keep secret."

"Whatever her reasons are, it's none of our business. We owe it to her to go along with her request."

Bettina sighed. "I guess you're right."

He nibbled suggestively on her ear, murmuring,

"Maybe we should tell them about the joys of matrimony."

"Nah." She put her arms around his neck and smiled alluringly. "It will be more fun when they find out for themselves."

Everybody else ceased to exist as David stripped off his towel and pulled his wife close.

Chapter Nine

Gianni had planned a dazzling week for Bettina and David. He took them inside St. Mark's Basilica and pointed out the breathtaking golden altarpiece encrusted with almost twenty-five hundred jewels.

They walked across the Bridge of Sighs while Gianni explained that it got its name because after sentencing, prisoners were marched across this bridge on their way to jail. He also told them what the guide books sometimes omitted, that Casanova was once held there, but escaped.

When their feet gave out and their minds went on overload from trying to take in all the unique and wonderful sights of Venice, Gianni took them someplace opulent for lunch. They drank wine and ate the local specialties like tiny fish fried in batter, rich, creamy risotto and for dessert, delicious cannoli.

"This is so fantastic!" Bettina exclaimed. "I don't know how we can ever thank you for all you've done for us."

"It's been really great." David added his thanks.

"Your enjoyment has made this week special for us, too, hasn't it, my love?" Gianni kissed Jillian's cheek.

"Yes, I wish it didn't have to end." She wished even more that he meant it when he called her his love.

"I refuse to think about leaving," Bettina declared. "We still have a couple of days left."

"And don't forget the masked ball," Jillian reminded her. "How's that for a grand finale?"

"I'm glad you reminded me," Gianni said. "We'd better do something about getting costumes for the three of you. Have you thought about what you want to wear?"

David grinned. "How about if Betts and I come as Adam and Eve? No muss, no fuss. All we have to do is pick a few fig leaves."

"I read somewhere that fig leaves are out this season," Bettina said. "Satin period gowns and powdered wigs are where it's at."

"You're not getting me into those fancy knickers with buckles at the knees," her husband stated.

As they bickered amicably, Gianni said to Jillian, "Who would you like to be?"

"Cinderella would be appropriate," she said.

When the ball ended, so would her romantic dreams for the future. Gianni's secretary would return to reclaim her job, and she wouldn't have any excuse to stay.

"How would anybody know you were Cinderella?" Bettina objected. "You'd just look like somebody in a ball gown—unless you know where to locate a pair of glass slippers."

"Why don't we wait and see what the costumers have to offer?" Gianni suggested. "We'll stop by there after lunch."

Picking out costumes took a lot longer than he anticipated. Gianni watched in amusement as Bettina tried on at least a dozen outfits, making up her mind only to change it repeatedly.

"Decide already!" David said. "It's only a party, not brain surgery."

"David's right," Jillian said. "If you don't choose something soon, we'll take a vote and do it for you."

"Oh sure, you can afford to be impatient," Bettina said in an injured tone. "You found the perfect costume right away."

"You can have it if you like. Anything to get us out of here! I have a final meeting with the florist in my office in half an hour."

"Okay, okay. I guess I'll go with the circus performer's outfit, and David can be a lion tamer."

"That was my choice an hour ago!" David exclaimed.

''I'll give you a piece of advice,'' Gianni chuckled. ''Don't argue when you get your own way.''

Jillian got back to her office with a few minutes to spare before her appointment, enough time to play the messages on the answering machine. None sounded particularly urgent except the ones from Gianni's secretary. She had called twice and requested that he call her back as soon as possible.

Jillian wondered what that was all about, but the florist arrived and she had to give him her full attention. He'd brought large charts showing which floral arrangements went in which rooms. They were all color coded to go with the decor. Some of the flowers he'd wanted to use were unavailable, so he needed her okay on the substitutions he proposed.

When Gianni had offered her the job, Jillian wondered if it was an act of charity. After all, how much work could be involved in giving a party? Even one this big. Now she knew. It was like coordinating a Broadway show.

Gianni appeared not long after the florist had left. ''Are there any problems I should know about?'' he asked.

''No, that's what you have me for.''

''And I know how fortunate I am.'' He lifted her chin in his palm and gazed at her with desire deep in his amber eyes.

''It's nice to know I'm appreciated.''

''I'm looking forward to showing you just how much, later tonight.''

''I'll be waiting.'' She took a deep breath to break the spell he could weave so effortlessly. ''You have two messages from your secretary.''

''Two? I hope nothing is wrong.'' He reached for the telephone.

Jillian left him alone to make his call and went upstairs to her room. Gianni joined her there a short time later.

''Is everything all right with Bella?'' she asked.

''I'm hoping it will be, but there's been another complication. The doctor wants to do a Cesarean section. He's afraid that prolonged labor might be dangerous for her and the baby.''

''That's too bad. But C-sections are quite common nowadays. I don't think she needs to worry.''

''I hope you're right. She won't be returning to work anytime soon, though. That's what she called to tell me. Would it be an imposition to ask you to stay on longer?''

Jillian stared at him, finding it difficult to believe she'd been given a gift of time. Her coach wasn't going to turn into a pumpkin after the ball!

''I realize you didn't come to Venice to do secretarial work,'' he said when she didn't answer. ''I'll call an agency and tell them to send me someone.''

''No! I mean, you don't have to do that,'' she said. ''I'll be glad to stay if you need me.''

''There isn't a time when I don't need you, *cara*.'' He took her in his arms and kissed her, gently at first, then with increasing passion. He was reaching for her back zipper when there was a knock and Bettina's voice sounded through the heavy door. Gianni's arms dropped to his sides and he sighed. "You know how fond I am of your sister. But she has the world's worst timing."

"Tell me about it! I grew up with her." Jillian laughed. "But they'll be going home soon with glowing reports about you. Try not to ruin your image now."

"All right, but it's going to cost you—starting tonight."

"Promise?" she teased as she went to answer the door.

The night of the ball finally arrived. Before going to get dressed, Jillian checked the house to make sure everything was perfect. Which it was. The large staff of artisans had done their jobs well.

Huge floral arrangements perfumed the living room and all of the reception rooms. More flowers in every color of the rainbow were twined around the banisters on both sides of the grand staircase. The entire villa looked like an indoor garden.

After checking out the downstairs, Jillian went up to the third floor ballroom. It had been transformed for the night into a medieval court. Banners in royal blue, crimson and gold hung from the lofty ceilings. The silk and satin banners were intricately embroidered with various coats of arms.

Each arriving guest would enter on a red velvet carpet and be announced with a trumpet fanfare by costumed pages. Suits of armor that had been worn by Gianni's distant ancestors stood in corners, and ancient weapons hung on the walls; ornamental maces, crossbows and the like.

Jillian gave everything a critical inspection. She even walked over to straighten a fold on one of the damask draperies looped back from the tall, sparkling clean windows that lined one wall. When she was certain that everything was perfection, she went to get dressed.

With all of that, she was still the first one who was ready. Gianni was walking around his bedroom in his briefs when she went to find him. The only other thing he had on was a gold medallion on a heavy gold chain, nestled among the springy hair on his broad chest.

"Do you realize your guests will be arriving practically any minute?" she gasped. "What am I going to do with you?"

"I have a suggestion." He walked over and tried to put his arms around her, but she eluded his grasp.

"There's no time for that."

"There's always time." His eyes kindled as he gazed at her. "*Mama mia,* do you look sexy! You're going to need a bodyguard when the men see you in that outfit."

Jillian had chosen a belly dancer's costume. The bra and the girdle of the brief panties were covered with coin-size gold paillettes. Attached to the girdle were filmy pantaloons made of a sheer white fabric. Around her bare shoulders she wore a long scarf of the same material. It veiled, but didn't conceal her alluring body.

"You're the one who's going to need protection if you go to the party looking like that," she said. "The women will mob you, and I don't need the competition."

"You don't have any." He cupped his hand around the back of her neck, under the soft spill of auburn hair and said in a husky voice, "How could I want any other woman after I've known you?"

"Oh, Gianni," she groaned. "Please put on some clothes!"

"All right," he laughed. "But you don't know what you're missing."

That was the trouble—she did! And it was very difficult to say no to him. Jillian waited until he'd zipped up the black silk pants of a gondolier and pulled on the striped jersey that went with the costume. Then she left the room and went downstairs.

She was talking to the chief of security about the placement of his men when Bettina and David joined her. They looked like tightrope walker Barbie and lion tamer Ken. She was adorable in a pink tutu with a skimpy satin top, and David looked very macho in fawn-colored breeches and a long whip.

"You'd better put on your masks," Jillian told them after they'd all exclaimed over each other's costumes. "The guests are starting to arrive."

They all moved to a window in an alcove and looked out. The dock was very festive with all the colored twinkling lights, flickering candles and garlands of flowers looped along the railing and striped docking poles. A red carpet that stretched from the landing all the way to the front door was also impressive.

"It looks like the setting for an outdoor wedding," Bettina remarked.

"Or a very friendly invasion," David said.

A flotilla of boats was streaming down the canal toward their pier. A couple of them had already docked and men dressed in feudal page's outfits were helping bejeweled women to disembark.

"Look at *that* costume!" Bettina exclaimed, staring avidly at a woman in an ornately embroidered green velvet gown with a very low-cut neckline. She was wearing an elaborately curled black wig and a great deal of jewelry. "I guess she's supposed to be Scarlett O'Hara. I wonder who she really is."

"Sylvie, the Countess of Rivoli," Jillian answered briefly.

"How can you tell when she's wearing a mask, and probably a wig?"

"There can't be two emerald necklaces like that. I've seen it on her before."

"You mean it's real?" David took a sharper look.

Jillian merely nodded. She was glancing around for Gianni. Was she supposed to act as hostess and greet the guests? Then she saw him coming down the stairs. He was recognizable even wearing a mask. Not many men had his lean, hard body and regal grace. She watched with a feeling of pride as he exchanged a few laughing words with the nearest men and kissed the hands of the women.

"Did you ever see such fabulous costumes?" Bettina and David were watching the arriving guests. "I don't know which are more fantastic, the outfits or the jewels," she said.

"Except for the character in the white loin cloth and the sheet around his shoulders," David said. "I'll bet it took a lot of convincing to get him into *that* outfit—whatever it is."

"He's supposed to be a swami. You should have paid attention in your comparative religions class."

"I learned enough to know that a grown man looks ridiculous in diapers." David grinned.

"I'd better go upstairs and tell the musicians to start playing," Jillian said. "Have fun. I'll see you later."

The guests were all milling around the rooms on the first floor. But after the music drifted down the staircase, a steady stream of people were drawn to the ballroom.

Two pages with long slender golden trumpets had taken their places by the door. Each guest was given a fanfare and announced. Most of the names were recognizable, and a great many were prestigious.

Waiters circulated around the ballroom with trays of champagne in crystal flutes, but there were also a couple of bars set up at opposite ends of the room. Both were busy.

The caterer's staff would soon be offering an elaborate selection of hot and cold hors d'oeuvres.

Jillian was about to call down to the kitchen and give the order to start serving, when a platoon of waiters arrived and fanned out through the room. The trays were works of art, she noticed approvingly. Shrimp and lobster canapés alternated with truffled pate, tiny baked potatoes topped with sour cream and caviar, and large olives stuffed with smoked oysters.

As she was completing her inspection a man came up to her. He was dressed as one of the three musketeers, she guessed, in an elaborate costume that included a wide-brimmed hat with a feathered plume.

"Don't tell me you eat any of those things," he remarked.

Jillian took it as a criticism and became defensive. "They're awfully good. You really should try one. Don't you see anything you like?"

"That's a leading question if ever I heard one." His avid glance swept over her as he took her hand and led her onto the dance floor. "What I meant was, I can't imagine that you eat earthly food. Not with that out-of-this-world figure. I'll bet I'm not the first man to tell you that you're the most gorgeous woman here."

"And *I'll* bet this isn't the first time tonight that you've used that line."

"Would a king lie?" he asked.

"Is that who you're supposed to be? I guessed wrong."

"Actually I'm supposed to be Don Juan, but I must not be doing it right."

Jillian could have told him he was *over*doing it. He was holding her too closely, and his caressing hands were wandering down her back. It made her especially uncomfortable since she was so skimpily dressed. Jillian knew how to discourage a man— firmly if necessary—but she didn't want to risk a scene. As usual, Gianni solved her problem.

Tapping the man on the shoulder, he said, "I'll take over now, Milos."

"I don't need any assistance." The man tried to sound as if he were joking, but he was clearly displeased by the interruption. "The lady and I were just getting acquainted."

"Don't worry, I'll tell her all about you," Gianni said smoothly. He took Jillian in his arms and led her into the other dancers. When they were out of earshot he remarked, "This is why Milos hangs onto his title. He thinks it gives him droit du seigneur."

"You mean he really *is* a king?" Jillian asked.

"*Was*—of a small country that abolished their monarchy many years ago. He doesn't mention that little fact, though, especially when he meets a beautiful woman."

"You didn't give him a chance to tell me. He was just getting warmed up."

"So I noticed." Gianni's lips brushed her temple. "The others are waiting for their turn. All the men here want to meet you. At least a dozen of them have asked me who you are."

Jillian hoped the interest of other men had made him jealous. ''I get the most attention because I have on the least amount of clothes,'' she said lightly.

''I'm looking forward to removing those later tonight,'' he murmured in her ear.

Gianni wasn't holding her as tightly as the other man had, but she was achingly conscious of him. The pliant muscles in his strong thighs were tantalizing when they brushed against hers, and the warmth of his hands through the thin chiffon that veiled her body fueled her need for him. As they were gazing into each other's eyes, a man dancing next to them clapped Gianni on the back.

He was an American, from Texas judging by his accent, but he was dressed as an English magistrate, complete with curly white wig. ''Great party, old buddy! You're gonna be a tough act to follow.''

Couples dancing nearby echoed his sentiments, and then the orchestra took a break and they all trailed off the dance floor. While Gianni was surrounded by his friends, Jillian slipped away to check that everything was running smoothly behind the scenes.

A couple of servants waited outside on the dock for latecomers, but it appeared that all the guests had arrived. She reassigned one of the servants, then went to the kitchen to see if all was well there. The massive kitchen looked chaotic, but that was deceptive. The well-trained workers knew exactly what they were doing and didn't need her underfoot.

As she started for the staircase, Jillian saw a flash

of movement in one of the reception rooms. She went to investigate and found a man dressed as a monk with a cowl over his head, shading his face. A guest, no doubt. But what was he doing down here all alone?

Jillian smiled brightly as she approached him. "Are you looking for someone? This house is so huge that it's easy to get lost."

"Yes, it— I was supposed to meet my wife here. At least I thought she said to meet her downstairs."

"She probably got tired of waiting. All the fun is upstairs. I'll walk up with you."

"That would be nice." The man didn't express doubts about abandoning his wife. "I didn't want to go into the ballroom alone."

"I've felt that way myself at big parties. You get the feeling that everyone is staring at you."

"Something like that."

"Evidently your wife doesn't feel the same way."

"I guess not." When they reached the ballroom he said, "I don't want to keep you from the party. I can look for her by myself."

Jillian didn't argue. She left him and went to find Alfredo, the chief of security. At first she couldn't locate him. She made a circuit of the large ballroom, then discovered he was outside in the hall with one of his men.

After telling him why she was uneasy about the man in the monk's outfit, he asked her to point him out. They found him kissing the hand of an older woman who was decked out in enough jewels to stock Tiffany's.

Alfredo moved in swiftly and took the man's arm in a firm grip. "Well, if it isn't my old friend, Nick! Imagine seeing you here."

"I'm afraid you've made a mistake," the man said. "My name is Hans...Hans Von Hofstein."

"Really? It's amazing how much you look like Nick." Alfredo signaled unobtrusively to one of his men. "Why don't we go outside and discuss it?"

"Some other time. I have just asked this charming lady to dance with me."

"I strongly urge you to change your mind."

The older woman was regarding them with a puzzled frown. "May I ask what this is all about?"

When Nick saw the other security guard converging on them, he gave the woman a slight bow. "Forgive me, dear lady, but I'm afraid we will have to postpone our dance."

Jillian accompanied the men out of the ballroom. When their little procession was in the outer hall, Alfredo patted the man down. Under his monk's robe, in a deep pocket of his baggy jeans, was a huge diamond ring and a sapphire-and-diamond bracelet.

"How did he steal those so fast?" Jillian gasped. "I only left him alone for a short time."

"That's all it takes a professional. They're quick and they're smooth. The mark doesn't even know she's been robbed until long after he's gone."

"I can't believe he could remove someone's jewelry without her feeling anything!'' Jillian exclaimed.

''Believe it.'' Nick grinned. ''If you'd given me about fifteen more minutes, I'd have been out of here with a big emerald necklace I spotted. I was working my way up to it.''

''The woman we found him with had a close call,'' Alfredo said. ''After he kissed her hand at the end of their dance, she would have been minus one of those big rings. You did a good job, Miss Colby. This guy could have gotten away with over a million dollars worth of jewels tonight.''

As the security guard put handcuffs on the thief, Nick said to Jillian, ''Where did I go wrong? What tipped you off?''

''Your running shoes, for one thing,'' she answered. ''You should have been wearing sandals. The jeans under your robe were a false note, too.''

Gianni came out of the ballroom as the guard was taking the man downstairs. ''What's going on?'' he asked.

After Jillian explained what happened, Alfredo told him how clever and potentially dangerous the jewel thief was. ''You can be very proud of this lady.''

As Gianni and Jillian were returning to the ballroom, he said to her, ''From now on you're just a guest at this party. I don't want you to take any more chances.''

''Alfredo was exaggerating. Jewel thieves aren't violent.''

"When did you get to be an authority on crime?" He tipped her chin up and gazed deeply into her eyes. "I don't know what I'd do if anything happened to you."

They were too engrossed in each other to notice Sylvie staring at them from a short distance away. Her expression was chilling.

The rest of the evening seemed to fly by. Gianni had to circulate among his guests, but Jillian wasn't alone. She danced almost every dance and met stimulating people.

At midnight everyone took off their masks. Most of the really famous guests had been recognizable, by their voices or distinctive mannerisms. But there were some surprises. A renowned Shakespearean actor had fooled everyone with his clown outfit.

While the guests were exclaiming over each other, servants were busy setting up tables for a midnight supper. The large round tables were covered with silver lamé cloths centered by bowls of white and pale green orchids nestled in leaves that had been sprayed with silver paint.

Beside each place setting was a box tied with either pink or blue satin ribbon. Pink for the ladies, blue for the men. The women were receiving gold compacts with a jeweled design on the lid. The men's party favor was a solid gold money clip.

When the pages sounded a call on their trumpets, everyone straggled over to the tables. After the guests were finally seated, Gianni walked out to a podium that had been placed in front of the orchestra. It was covered with a blanket of velvety white gardenias that perfumed the room.

The pages blew their trumpets again to quiet everyone, and Gianni formally welcomed his guests and made a few humorous remarks. Then, to Jillian's surprise, he called her up to the stage.

Taking her hand, he said, "If you have enjoyed yourselves this evening, much of the credit goes to this lovely lady, Jillian Colby. She has my undying gratitude. I couldn't have done it without her."

While the other guests applauded, two women at Bettina and David's table discussed their host's surprising announcement.

"Sylvie isn't going to like that," one of them commented. "I've never known Gianni to call attention to his interest in a woman. He's such a private person."

The other woman shrugged. "She's just his latest fling. He can't be serious about her. She's an American, a nobody."

Bettina flushed and drew in her breath sharply, but David squeezed her arm. "Don't go ballistic," he warned.

"Forget it! I'm not going to let them talk about my sister that way."

"You won't be doing her any favor by making a scene."

Bettina knew he was right, but she was steaming as the women continued to gossip.

"When Gianni gets ready to settle down, he'll go back to Sylvie," the woman continued.

"She'd be a suitable wife," her friend agreed. "But I'm not sure he was ever serious about her. You know how men are. They date a woman for a while and then they lose interest and move on to the next one."

"He won't get rid of Sylvie that easily. She'll do whatever it takes to get him back."

Their conversation ended when a parade of waiters marched in carrying the first course, wild mushroom soup ladled into small round loaves of hollowed-out French bread.

Bettina's face was troubled as she turned to her husband and said in a low voice, "Do you think Gianni is just playing games with Jill? I never bought her reasons for keeping their engagement a secret. I didn't even understand them."

"Well, I guess it makes sense to them. It's their lives, you know."

"Maybe so, but I can't help worrying about her. Gianni's intentions aren't the only question mark. I wonder if she knows that countess with the emeralds hasn't given up on him."

David sighed. "I don't suppose you'd listen if I told you to stay out of it."

A grin lightened Bettina's troubled expression for a moment. "See how well you know me after only a few weeks of marriage?"

After the elaborate midnight supper was over, the tables were swiftly cleared away and the orchestra began to play again, disco music this time. The ball would last until the early hours of the morning, when breakfast would be served.

Bettina left David and went to look for her sister. She found her talking to a group of people in especially inventive costumes. One rather gruesome trio were Dracula, Frankenstein and the Werewolf of London.

Jillian introduced her sister and then said to her, "Where were you? Gianni and I wanted you and David to sit at our table."

"We couldn't find you, so we just picked a table. It's a good thing, too. Can I talk to you for a minute? Alone."

"What's up?" Jillian asked as they strolled outside onto a balcony where the noise of the crowd was muted.

Her face sobered when she heard what Bettina had to tell her, but she pretended to shrug it off. "You know how some busybodies like to gossip. It doesn't mean anything."

"I hope not, but just to be on the safe side, I think you should announce your engagement. This would be a perfect time. Let everybody know Gianni is taken."

"No! Not tonight. Promise me you won't say anything!"

After a moment's hesitation, Bettina said, "All right, I promise, but something isn't right. What have you gotten yourself into, Jill? You can tell me. I'm your best friend."

"You're letting your imagination run riot. Everything is fine. Just relax and enjoy yourself. Isn't it a marvelous party?''

Bettina brushed that aside. "Okay, but tell me one thing. Is Gianni exerting some kind of pressure on you, or are you truly in love with him?''

"Those are two questions," Jillian said with a slight laugh.

"And you haven't answered either of them."

Jillian chose her words carefully. "Gianni is as wonderful as he appears. We have something very special together." That was the truth, even if it wasn't the whole truth. She could only hope Bettina wouldn't analyze her answer.

She didn't have time to. A couple of men spotted them on the balcony and insisted they come inside and dance.

It was almost five in the morning before the last guest left, after a buffet breakfast.

"They're like babies that need frequent feedings," Jillian commented as she and Gianni walked down the staircase hand in hand. "I don't know how any of them could eat again after that marvelous midnight supper. I don't want to look at food for a week!"

"I'll remind you of that at lunchtime tomorrow."

He would have walked with her down the hall, but she stopped at the door to his suite. "I'm sure Bettina and David will sleep till at least noon. And when they do get up, they'll have more on their minds than checking out our sleeping arrangements.''

"You're going to stay with me tonight?" he asked with a pleased expression.

"What there is left of it. It's dawn."

When they went inside she drifted over to one of the tall windows and gazed out. A strip of lavender merging into rose separated the dark water of the canal from the slate-gray sky. A few boats were out, but the normally busy water was calm enough to reflect the domes and spires of the surrounding churches.

"It's so calm and peaceful at this hour." Jillian was filled with contentment as she rested her head on Gianni's shoulder. He was standing behind her with his arms around her waist.

"A perfect time to make love," he murmured, nuzzling her ear.

"You say that no matter what time it is," she teased.

"Does it bother you?" He removed the gauzy scarf from around her shoulders so he could caress her bare skin.

"Yes, it drives me wild," she said with a smile, pulling the shirt out of his slacks.

"That was my intention."

Their eyes held as they undressed each other slowly. Her spangled bra was discarded on the floor, followed by his striped jersey. They stroked each other sensuously, prolonging the pleasure.

"This is what I've been looking forward to all

night,'' Gianni said in a husky voice. ''You're so beautiful. I can't believe you're mine.''

''Are you mine?'' she asked, sliding her palms over his broad chest.

''Darling Jillian! How can you doubt it?''

She didn't—at that moment. Gianni was as hungry for her as she was for him. Their lovemaking gradually quickened in tempo. When their costumes were lying in a heap on the carpet, they explored each other's nude bodies, knowing from experience what was most arousing.

The liquid fire that was centered in their loins soon mounted to a fever pitch, demanding to be satisfied. They were both so taut with desire that they sank to the carpet, arms and legs intertwined, whispering heated words of passion.

The rising sun smiled through the window at them and turned their straining, glistening bodies to gold. They reached nirvana as the city awakened to a new beginning.

Afterward, lying in Gianni's arms in bed, Jillian was completely relaxed. The doubts and fears that Bettina had raised were gone. It was foolish to question Gianni's love, even if he hadn't ever put it into words. His actions spoke for him.

He pulled her closer with a small sound of contentment. ''This is nice, knowing you're going to be here like this in the morning. Do you think we could make it a regular occurrence?''

''It's a distinct possibility,'' Jillian answered happily.

Chapter Ten

Everybody slept late on the day after the ball. Then they all gathered around a table in the garden for a late lunch. The main topic of conversation was of course, the previous night's gala event. Gianni listened indulgently as Jillian and her sister and brother-in-law excitedly discussed every detail of the ball: the costumes, the jewels and the famous guests.

"I can't wait to tell everybody at home that I danced with a prince and two movie stars!" Bettina exclaimed.

David groaned. "That's as bad as making people sit through home movies of your vacation. Nobody is really interested. Promise you'll only tell the story once."

"Once to everybody we know," she agreed.

"I'm glad you enjoyed yourselves," Gianni said.

"It's been the greatest trip ever! I hate to go home."

"You can always come back. The welcome mat will be out."

"You're a darling, and we'll be happy to take you up on that invitation." Bettina slanted a glance at her sister. "We'll be back for your wedding, naturally."

"I thought this trip took all of your ready cash," Jillian said, feeling her body tense. Bettina was like a bulldog; she just wouldn't let go. "Where will you get the airfare?"

"The good old American way." Bettina laughed. "We'll put it on our credit cards. I certainly don't intend to miss your wedding." She turned to Gianni and asked artlessly, "Do you have any kind of date in mind? I mean, Jill said you were going to discuss it after the ball was over."

"It hasn't been twenty-four hours yet!" Jillian exclaimed.

David pushed back his chair and said to his wife, "Come on, you'd better start to pack."

"I have plenty of time. We're not leaving until tomorrow."

"Now, Betts," he said quietly.

She got up without further argument.

After they'd gone into the house, Gianni said, "I misjudged that young man. He's firm when it counts."

"Yes, David is a dear. Bettina can be somewhat overpowering, but he'll hold his own with her." After a moment of silence, Jillian said, "I'm sorry she tried to back you into a corner about the wedding."

"I'm a big boy. I can take care of myself."

It wasn't the answer she was looking for. "Well, thank goodness we just have to hang in there a little longer." She put her napkin on the table and stood. "I think I'll go and see if I can help them pack."

Gianni's expression was inscrutable as he watched her leave.

Her sister's visit had put a strain on Jillian at times, but she felt let-down after they'd put the young couple on the plane.

Gianni reached out and snaked an arm around her waist, drawing her to his side as he steered the power boat down the Grand Canal. "Are you feeling homesick?"

"I suppose that's partly it."

"What else is bothering you, *cara?* Tell me and I'll fix it."

"Like you fixed all my other problems? You must be getting pretty tired of them." She tried to pull away, but his arm tightened.

"How could I ever tire of you?" he crooned. "You brighten my days and make my nights an endless delight."

She wasn't in the mood for compliments. "You Italians are very good with words."

He looked at her searchingly. "This is more serious than being homesick, isn't it? Did I do or say something to upset you last night? We were up and out early this morning, so it couldn't have been something that happened today.''

Gianni had taken them to the best restaurant in Venice for a gala farewell dinner the night before. Then they'd gone to a little club that had entertainment. He had also given Bettina and David costly parting gifts, a beautiful Florentine gold watch for each of them. When they protested that he was being too generous, Gianni said it was his wedding gift to them.

Jillian was ashamed of her shrewish behavior when she was reminded of what a nice person Gianni was. It wasn't his fault that he didn't love her.

''I'm sorry for being so cranky,'' she said in a chastened voice. ''I guess you can blame it on the fact that I've been running on adrenaline for so long and now it's all over—the ball, my job. You could manage on your own until Bella comes back. You don't really need me, do you, Gianni?''

''How can you even ask such a thing?''

''That's no answer. You know what I'm talking about. I'd like to think I'm being paid solely for my expertise in the office.''

He gave her a shocked look. ''That's insulting to both of us!''

''I have to know.''

''I shouldn't have to tell you. Didn't I thank you publicly for all your hard work? I meant it when I said the ball wouldn't have been the same without you."

"I'm talking about now, Gianni. Is there really anything left for me to do?"

"You'll probably ask for a raise when you see how much. I intended to give you a few days to rest up before going back to work, but the bills for the party need to be paid, none of my correspondence has been answered for a week, and the paperwork on your desk looks like a blizzard hit. That's just to start with."

"Yes, I know the office is a mess. After Bettina and David got here I let some of the nonessentials slide so I could spend time with them. The filing did pile up pretty badly. I'll get on it right away."

Jillian's nagging doubts were eased. She couldn't have stayed on and accepted money from Gianni unless they had a valid business arrangement. Yet how could she ever bear to leave him?

He looked heartbreakingly handsome standing at the wheel with his dark hair tossed by the wind. She gazed at his chiseled profile, the high, aristocratic cheekbones, the firm mouth that softened against hers when they made love.

He turned his head and smiled at her, and Jillian smiled back. This man was the love of her life—and always would be. That was the only sure thing in her uncertain future.

Gianni had always led an active social life, but it intensified after the ball. He was bombarded with invitations from friends who wanted to reciprocate, and he took Jillian to all the parties. Her life was as busy after the ball as it had been before—with a few important differences.

For one thing, she gave up her hotel room and moved to Gianni's villa. They spent every night together, making love, but also enjoying the close companionship of two people who were friends as well as lovers.

On the rare nights that they were free, they often had dinner served in Gianni's suite and then curled up on the couch together, listening to music or just talking. Those were the times that Jillian cherished.

During the day she was busy organizing Gianni's office. It was hopelessly outdated. Now that she had the time, she created a database for his foundation and entered it into the computer. Any files he might need were now readily accessible.

"I don't know how you functioned before this," she said, showing him what she'd done. "You'll be amazed at how much time you'll save. Everything you need is right here at the click of a mouse."

"Does it have another name?" Gianni chuckled. "Bella doesn't trust computers to begin with. She's certainly not going to touch something called a mouse."

Jillian was abruptly reminded that she was on borrowed time when he mentioned his secretary. "How is Bella feeling?"

"A little stressed, no doubt. She's anxious to have the baby. The operation is scheduled for next Mon-

day, and then of course she'll need time to recuper-
ate.''

"I'm sure she has the best doctors,'' Jillian said,
knowing Gianni was no doubt paying the bill. "She
and the baby should be just fine. And if the computer panics her when she comes back to work, I'll
be glad to walk her through it.''

"Did anyone ever tell you that you're a very nice
person?''

"Not lately.''

"That's going to change,'' he promised.

Jillian was glad that she'd had the foresight to ask
Bettina to bring some of her evening clothes, since
all the parties they attended were dressy. Sylvie was
at many of the larger affairs, always wearing a designer gown and decked out in jewels. Jillian didn't
envy her. She had Gianni.

One night when they were going to a dinner dance
at one of the luxury hotels, he asked her to wear a
pale yellow silk gown he'd seen on her before. Jillian was happy to please him, although the request
was unusual. All the other nights he had just told
her how beautiful she looked, no matter what she
was wearing.

The yellow silk was becoming with her auburn
hair and blue eyes. It was a simple dress that clung
to her figure alluringly. "How do I look?'' she
asked, anticipating his unfailing compliment.

This night Gianni surprised her. Gazing at her
critically he said, "I think it needs something.'' He

brought a square velvet jeweler's box out of his breast pocket and handed it to her.

She opened the box curiously, then gasped. Inside, on a bed of white satin, was a magnificent sunburst pin. Rays of diamonds in varying lengths surrounded a large yellow stone that looked like a sparkling sun. Surely it wasn't a canary diamond! But Jillian had a feeling it was.

"I can't accept this, Gianni! It's much too expensive."

"It isn't polite to mention the cost of a gift." He took the box from her and fastened the pin to the shoulder of her gown.

She protested vigorously until he put a finger on her lips. "It's little enough, considering all you've done for me."

"I haven't done anything. It's the other way around."

"No, *cara mia,* you brought sunshine into my life. I'm just sharing it with you."

Her eyes glistened with tears at the lovely sentiment. "That's the nicest thing anyone has ever said to me. I don't know how to thank you."

"Your pleasure is more than enough. Do you really like the pin? If you'd prefer something else you can exchange it. I won't mind."

What she really would have preferred was a plain gold ring, but Jillian assured him that she was thrilled with his gift.

All the women at the dinner dance noticed it immediately and asked if it was new. Jillian hadn't worn any noteworthy jewelry before this. She confirmed that it was new, and let it go at that. Let them draw their own conclusions.

The subject was discussed behind her back. The consensus of opinion was that Gianni had given it to her, and it was a sign that he was really serious this time. But some of the women disagreed.

"He's obviously mad about her, but that doesn't mean he's finally ready to get married," one said.

"That's a pretty expensive friendship gift," another remarked dryly.

"You know how generous Gianni is—and how rich. The money means nothing to him."

Another in the group nodded her head. "This isn't the first expensive gift he's given to a woman, and it won't be the last."

They argued about his intentions, but most of his friends agreed that he and Jillian were a stunning couple who seemed made for each other.

Not everybody concurred. Sylvie had her own supporters, especially two women named Tina and Isabel, who were happy to offer her their advice.

As they watched Gianni smiling fondly at some remark of Jillian's, Isabel said, "Gianni is making a fool of himself over that woman. If you don't do something, she's liable to trap him into marriage."

"Don't be ridiculous!" Sylvie frowned. "He's just amusing himself with her. It doesn't take a rocket scientist to know what he wants from her—and it isn't marriage."

"You never can tell. They seem very smitten with

each other. Have you seen the way she looks at him? Men are always flattered when a woman thinks they're perfect.''

"For a while perhaps.'' Sylvie shrugged. "And then that mindless adulation gets tiresome and they look for someone more stimulating.''

"It's surprising that she's lasted this long. American women don't know how to handle Italian men,'' Tina remarked.

Isabel nodded in agreement. "They make a fuss over the slightest thing. Their relationship will be in trouble if Jillian thinks Gianni is paying too much attention to another woman. I'll bet she has the temper that goes with that red hair.''

"And men hate it when women make a scene,'' Tina said.

Sylvie looked thoughtful. "Let's see just how well she handles a challenge.''

Her friends watched, smiling in anticipation as she left them and sauntered over to the group where Gianni and Jillian were standing.

Sylvie put her hand on Gianni's arm and said, "Can I speak to you for a minute?''

"Of course,'' he said pleasantly.

"I meant alone.'' She turned to Jillian. "You don't mind if I steal him away, do you?''

"Not as long as you bring him back.'' Jillian smiled at Gianni rather than the other woman.

Sylvie clung to his arm and guided him toward the French doors leading outside. Gianni gave her a quizzical look, but didn't object.

When they reached the garden, which was deserted, he said, "Whatever you have to tell me must be top secret if we need this much privacy."

She slanted a glance at him. "Perhaps I just wanted to be alone with you. Remember that night in Monte Carlo when we left a party like this and went for a walk along the beach?"

"You have a good memory."

"It isn't easy to forget things like that. We had some good times together, didn't we, darling?"

"Yes, you're a very lovely lady," he said gently.

"We could have them again. Nothing has changed."

"Things always change. It's the nature of life. But this is no place to discuss it. We'd better go inside. It's too cool out here for you. I'm afraid you'll catch cold."

"No, wait! I really do want to discuss something with you. I guess I got sidetracked by nostalgia." She gave a little laugh and then continued hurriedly, "It's about the meeting of the Worldwide Children's Fund in Paris. I'm going as one of the delegates, and this is all new to me. Since the conference will be coming up soon, I wanted to ask if you could give me some literature to read. You know, about the work the organization is doing and where aid is most urgently needed. I want to be able to cast my vote intelligently."

"I didn't know you were interested in childrens' causes." Gianni gave her his unfeigned attention.

"I wasn't when we were going together. But

lately I've become aware of all the terrible things that are happening in the world. You can't read about those poor little victims without wanting to get involved.''

''I think that's splendid! I have a statistical report that's just what you're looking for. There are some other things you should read, too. Let me jot them down for you.''

Sylvie took a small jeweled pen out of her evening purse, and Gianni searched his pockets for a scrap of paper as they moved toward a patio table and chairs.

Jillian had been amused at the other woman's transparent threat to take Gianni away from her. Sylvie's timing couldn't have been worse. How could she, Jillian, feel insecure after Gianni's magnificent gift and moving compliment just hours earlier?

Her smile was genuine as she chatted and sipped champagne with the other guests. But as time passed, Jillian became a little annoyed at Gianni. Sylvie would try to keep him all to herself as long as possible, but he didn't have to cooperate. There were limits to how much courtesy was required!

At least half an hour passed before they returned. Gianni came to look for her immediately, but by then, Jillian had trouble hiding her irritation. The smug look on Sylvie's face irked her even more.

Gianni explained what they had been talking about, and Sylvie apologized sweetly for keeping him so long. Jillian was sure he didn't see the sparkle of malice in the woman's eyes. Men were so clueless, she thought disgustedly, even sophisticated men like Gianni.

Jillian managed to hide her displeasure, although she was sure Sylvie was aware of it. But the other woman left him alone from then on, and the rest of the evening passed pleasantly.

Gianni was satisfactorily ardent when they returned home after the party. They made love with passion and tenderness. Jillian hadn't mentioned the countess's name, but as they relaxed in each other's arms she decided now was a good time.

"I can understand why your former girlfriends don't want to let you go," she began. "You're slightly terrific."

"Only slightly?" he teased.

"Did Sylvie give you a higher rating?"

"A gentleman doesn't kiss and tell," he countered in a light tone.

"That's an admission of guilt." Jillian tried for the same light touch, but couldn't quite bring it off.

"The only thing I'm guilty of is being addicted to you. Other women don't exist for me." He wrapped his arms and legs more tightly around her and urged her body closer to his. "Can't you tell?"

He murmured erotic words in her ear as he tickled and teased in all the right places. For one of their few times together, Jillian really would have preferred to talk. She tried to resist him, but it was useless. Gianni could always drive everything else from her mind with his clever hands and seductive mouth.

They made love as if for the first time. When he entered her, their cries of ecstasy mounted in intensity as they rocked against each other, striving for the ultimate moment of rapture. The burst of sensation welded their bodies together when it came.

Much later, when Gianni had fallen asleep in her arms, Jillian realized how foolish she'd been to worry about Sylvie. How much more proof did she need that he loved *her,* even if he didn't say so? One day—hopefully soon—he would conquer his fear of commitment and tell her what she ached to hear.

A couple of days later, Bettina phoned, ostensibly to tell Jillian that she and David had found *the* perfect apartment right near the campus. They discussed it for a few minutes, then Bettina gave her the latest news about family and friends.

Finally she got around to asking what she really wanted to know. "So…have you and Gianni set a date for your wedding yet?"

"We've been on the go so much that we haven't had a moment to discuss it. You wouldn't believe what our social life is like!"

"It seems to me your wedding would take priority over that."

"There really isn't any hurry."

"No, I suppose not. I'm sure Gianni wouldn't mind waiting indefinitely."

"I can do without your sarcasm," Jillian said tartly.

"I'm merely telling it like it is. Men aren't in any hurry to give up the bachelor life—especially when they're enjoying the status quo so much."

"You're implying that Gianni is taking advantage of me, but you're wrong. You met him. How can you think a thing like that? He's the sweetest, most thoughtful man in the world!"

"I couldn't agree more—but he's still a man. If you don't push for the gold ring, you might not get it."

"Is that what you did with David? I noticed he went down that aisle a little reluctantly," Jillian joked, hoping to distract her sister.

It didn't work. "You and Gianni aren't like us. Gianni is older and more sophisticated than David."

"What does that have to do with it?"

"He's more experienced at evading the trap." Bettina laughed, then grew serious again. "I don't want to see you get hurt, Jill. If you really love him, don't let your relationship get stuck in neutral."

Jillian had all but forgotten her original game plan—that she would eventually announce that she was breaking up with Gianni. During these last weeks the plan had seemed unnecessary. But he hadn't yet mentioned any kind of permanent arrangement. If it was all just wishful thinking on her part, she'd better stop baring her feelings for Gianni.

"Jill?" Bettina sounded chastened. "Don't be angry at me. I just want you and Gianni to be happy together.''

''Well, actually that's the problem. There have been times lately when I'm not sure we're right for each other.''

''You've got to be kidding! You just told me he's the greatest thing since air-conditioning in the tropics!''

''He is, but nobody is perfect. Gianni has some mannerisms that are really annoying.''

''We all do. He probably feels the same way about you, but he's too polite to mention it.''

''Exactly. That's why I don't think we should rush into marriage.''

''I can't believe you're looking for absolute perfection in a man! Do you know what you're going to wind up as?'' Bettina demanded. ''One of those little old ladies who gives her cats fancy names— all twelve of them!''

The conversation had turned painful for Jillian. ''If you don't mind, I'd prefer not to discuss it anymore. You only get to live *your* life, not mine, too.''

Both of them were troubled after they hung up.

Gianni noticed immediately when he came into the office. ''What's wrong, darling?''

''Nothing.'' She gave him a bright smile. ''I was just concentrating on something.''

He lifted her chin in his hand and kissed her sweetly. ''You don't have to tell me if you don't want to, but I know when something is bothering you.''

She sighed. "You're right. Bettina called and we had a slight disagreement."

"That's surprising. You get along so well together. What did you argue about?"

"Nothing important." Jillian managed a smile. "Now that she's married, Bettina thinks she's qualified to tell me how to run my life."

"Is there something wrong with your life?"

"Of course not! That's what is so aggravating. But I guess I'd better call her back and apologize."

"Do it later. You've been working too hard. Why don't you take a walk and smell the roses? I'd go with you, but I'm expecting a phone call."

"That's all right, I think I'll go shopping. I do feel like getting out for a while."

"I shouldn't have to tell you to take a break," he scolded. "Go out and enjoy yourself."

Did he have to be so caring? Jillian asked herself somberly as she walked toward St. Mark's Square a few minutes later. Life would be empty without him. The thought was so painful that she refused to consider the possibility.

Why not think positively instead? When she came home, Gianni would be waiting for her. He would be tender and loving, and they would live happily ever after.

At least she could count on three out of four of those things coming true, she told herself mockingly.

Chapter Eleven

Jillian really did need to go shopping. It wasn't just an excuse to get away from her troubles. The dresses Bettina had brought her from home were sufficient for a while, but she'd worn them over and over again. The other women seemed to have a new outfit for every party. Jillian couldn't hope to compete with them, but it was time to expand her wardrobe.

Money was no problem, for once. Gianni was paying her an excellent salary, and she'd saved most of it. Since she'd been living at his house, she had virtually no expenses.

Many of the famous designers had boutiques in Venice. They were filled with beautiful—and expensive!—merchandise, primarily for the tourist trade. Jillian had no intention of paying their kind of prices, but she always loved to browse through the lovely things.

A favorite of hers was a famous Italian designer who had shops all over the world. He was known for making elegant shoes and handbags, but he also designed classic sportswear. Jillian always stopped in there when she had the time.

The store was crowded this afternoon as usual, with foreign tourists speaking a variety of languages. They were buying all the things that had the designer's double initial logo on them, but Jillian bypassed those in favor of some classic cashmere sweaters in pastel colors.

She didn't notice the two women standing to one side. They had seen her come in, but they didn't go over to say hello. Isabel and Tina, Sylvie's best friends, merely watched her impassively.

"What is she doing here in the middle of the afternoon?" Tina said. "I thought she was supposed to be working for Gianni."

"Don't be dense, darling." Isabel gave a little trill of laughter. "She works the night shift."

"Personally, I wouldn't consider that work."

"Don't even think about it! Sylvie would snatch you bald."

"I meant, if Sylvie can't rekindle their romance. I wouldn't dream of jeopardizing my friendship with her."

"Tell that to somebody who will believe you. We'd all kill for a chance at Gianni!" Isabel said.

Their interest in Jillian intensified when they saw a man making his way toward her. He was the kind of man that women noticed, as much for the rakish air about him as his good looks.

"Jillian? I thought that was you!" he exclaimed as she whirled around. "I saw you through the window, and I knew there couldn't be two women with that glorious auburn hair."

"Hello, Rinaldo," she said in a tepid voice. Jillian had always known there was a possibility that she might run into him sooner or later in a place as small as Venice. She'd thought it would upset her, but it didn't. All she felt was distaste.

"*Cara mia,* this is like a dream come true! I was sure you had gone back to America. I went to your hotel when I thought you'd be ready to make up, but the desk clerk said you had checked out. Where did you go? Where have you been living all this time?"

The two women watching them looked at each other with a smirk. "How do you tell your old boyfriend that you hooked a bigger fish?" Tina murmured.

"I don't think that concerns you," Jillian said to him.

"I need to know. Everything about you is important to me, *mi amore.* You can't imagine what I went through." Rinaldo's voice throbbed with emotion. "I thought I had lost you forever."

"You have." She might eventually have gotten over her bitterness about what had happened on their wedding day, but even then she'd thought he was weak rather than evil. After reading the detective's report and discovering how really despicable he was, Jillian didn't want to be anyplace near him. "It's over, Rinaldo," she said flatly.

"You don't mean that. Not after the magical time we spent together."

"Including that last day in the church?"

He waved his hand as though brushing away an annoying fly. "That was regrettable, I'll admit, but it doesn't need to destroy our romance. The matter has been settled."

"How?" she asked bluntly. "Even *you* couldn't sweet-talk yourself out of that one."

"Don't worry your pretty little head about it. I took care of everything."

"I'm not worried because it doesn't concern me. You can do whatever you like with your life, as long as you leave me out of it."

"Ah, you are still angry," he said sadly. Then his face brightened. "But you still have feelings for me. A man knows these things."

"You have the hide of a rhinoceros! How can I convince you that I don't want anything more to do with you?"

"I'll never accept that. We were in love. Our hearts were joined. Have you forgotten how you melted in my arms as we watched the sun come up?"

The two eavesdropping women sidled closer so

they wouldn't miss a word. They were confident that Jillian was too absorbed to notice them.

"That isn't an accurate picture of our relationship, but you're so out of touch with reality that it's useless to argue with you." Jillian started for the door.

Rinaldo moved in front of her, blocking her path. "We have to talk."

"I have nothing to say to you, and I don't want to hear anything *you* have to say."

"Just give me a few minutes," he pleaded. "Have a drink with me."

"No." She tried to push past him, but he caught her arm.

"Coffee, then. I can't let it end like this. I love you, Jillian."

"Will you please lower your voice?" She was conscious of people staring at them. "You're making a scene."

"I don't care. I want the whole world to hear." He raised his voice. "Listen to me, all of you! This woman is breaking my heart. I love her, but she won't even let me talk to her!"

"Oh, Lord," Jillian muttered, turning red. People were not only staring, they were starting to snicker. "All right, I'll have coffee with you. Just keep quiet until we get out of here."

As Jillian marched out of the store with a stormy face, Isabel said to her friend, "Isn't the power of suggestion funny? I suddenly feel the urge for a cup of coffee."

"Wonderful idea!" Tina laughed.

They followed the other couple back to St. Mark's Square, where Rinaldo took the last vacant table on the perimeter of the busy quadrangle. All the tables surrounding it were filled with people drinking cappuccinos and watching the activity in the square, or reading the daily newspaper.

"Damn!" Tina exclaimed in annoyance. "We won't be close enough to hear anything."

"Let's take this table back here anyway," Isabel said. "At least we'll be able to see if they get romantic."

"You're joking! Jillian wasn't exactly glad to see him—in spite of that amazing announcement of his."

"Well, that told us he isn't just a casual acquaintance." Isabel snickered. "Who do you think he is?"

Tina shrugged. "Nobody important. I've never seen him at any of the places our crowd goes to."

"I wonder if she told Gianni about her fling with one of the local boys."

"Gianni certainly has a right to know. Maybe Sylvie could mention it to him. Oh, look!" Tina exclaimed. "They're holding hands."

That was only partially true. Rinaldo had taken Jillian's hand, but she pulled it away. "I said I'd have coffee with you—only because I had no choice. But this is really pointless," she said.

"Please, Jillian, I'm begging you for another chance. I know I should have told you about Maria and the baby, but I was afraid of losing you. Maria and I were never in love. It was just one of those things.''

''I don't doubt that, but she's the one who wound up with a baby. If you marry anybody, it should be Maria.''

''She doesn't want to get married. She just wants child support.''

''I thought you told me you were taking care of the baby.''

''I intended to. Maria didn't have to make that shocking scene. In church, of all places!'' He clearly considered himself the injured party.

''Too bad you never had a decent impulse in your life, Rinaldo. If you'd fulfilled your obligation, we'd be married right now.'' Jillian's tone was derisive, but she shuddered to think of what a close call she'd had.

An ugly look of anger and frustration transformed his face, before being quickly masked. His voice was muted as he said, ''I've made mistakes. I'm not perfect—I'll admit that. But I love you, and I know you still love me. I'll spend my life making you happy if you'll just give me the chance.''

Jillian sighed. ''I was never in love with you, Rinaldo. I was in love with the romance of Venice. I see that now.''

''We can recapture the romance. Venice is still the same.''

''But I'm not. I've fallen in love with someone else. Only this time it's the real thing.''

He looked at her sharply. "You're just saying that to discourage me."

"No, it's true."

The softened look on her face shook his confidence. "Where did you meet him? Who is this man?" he demanded.

"His name doesn't matter."

"Because there isn't anyone." He looked relieved. "You just made him up."

"I didn't invent someone to get even, or to make you jealous. You're so used to mistrusting people that you don't recognize the truth when you hear it." She pushed back her chair and stood. "Goodbye, Rinaldo. If it's any consolation, I'll never forget you."

The other two women stared avidly as Jillian walked away while Rinaldo sat there and simply watched her go.

"What do you think happened?" Isabel asked. "It doesn't look as if they made up."

"They didn't appear to be arguing, though," Tina said. "Maybe they made a date to meet someplace else."

"Why didn't they just leave together?"

"That wouldn't be discreet, since she's living with Gianni. Oh yes, look! He's getting up to go after her. I'll bet they have a secret love nest on one of those little streets nobody can find. Wouldn't you love to know?"

Isabel looked doubtful. "I can't walk that far in these spike heels."

"It doesn't matter. We've done our part. Let's go have a word with Sylvie."

Rinaldo's behavior would have surprised the two women, if they'd decided to follow him. He went in the same direction Jillian was headed, but he made sure to stay behind little groups of people, as though he didn't want her to see him.

It was easy for him to blend into the crowd near the square, but he was more visible when she reached Gianni's neighborhood of elegant palazzos. Only a sprinkling of people, mostly tourists taking pictures of the grand facades, were strolling along the worn cobblestones.

Rinaldo stayed close to the buildings, ready to duck out of sight if Jillian looked over her shoulder. Which she didn't. Even knowing all she did about him, Jillian wouldn't have believed that Rinaldo would stoop low enough to spy on her.

When she went up to the front door of Gianni's villa, he looked puzzled. These were the private homes of the privileged. Was it possible she'd gotten a job as a maid, or some other kind of servant? Had he wasted his time on the wrong mark? Maybe Jillian had told the truth when she said she didn't come from a wealthy family. Then a butler answered the door and bowed slightly as he stood aside to admit her.

Rinaldo's eyes started to gleam. "I *wasn't* wrong about her," he said softly. "I have a feeling little Jillian is going to make me a rich man—one way or another."

*   *   *

Gianni had gone out soon after Jillian left, but he came home before she did. He was glancing through the afternoon mail before going upstairs to take a shower. When the doorbell rang he assumed it was Jillian. He managed to mask his disappointment with a smile when Marco showed Sylvie into the den.

"This is a nice surprise," Gianni remarked.

"I just took a chance that I'd catch you at home. I got tired of waiting for you to call. The Worldwide Children's Fund conference is next week and we still haven't gotten together to discuss it as you promised," she said with the suggestion of a pout.

"I sent over some material for you to read. Didn't you get it?"

"Yes, and it was very helpful. But it didn't answer all my questions. I want to appear knowledgeable if I'm asked my opinion on anything."

Gianni hesitated. "Perhaps you can read over the latest committee report while I take a quick shower. I'm rather sweaty from tennis."

"I find that sexy in a man," Sylvie drawled. Her eyes moved deliberately over the tanned column of his throat, visible through his open polo shirt, down to his brief white shorts and strong legs.

Gianni didn't react. "All right, I suppose my shower can wait if you're sure you don't mind. Can I get you something to drink?" He tugged on the bell pull to summon the butler.

"I think I'll have champagne to celebrate."

"What are we celebrating? Is it something I should know about?"

"You will, darling, in due time." She smiled. "Now, about the conference. Will we have a car and driver at our disposal in Paris?"

"Will that influence any opinion you're asked to give?" He returned her smile, but his voice had a slight edge.

"No, of course not. I just thought we should get the unimportant details out of the way so we can concentrate on the things that really matter. Like fund-raising, for instance. Are we tapping all the potential sources?"

Gianni's reserve vanished, and his face became animated as they discussed a cause dear to his heart. Sylvie was a receptive audience. If she had few ideas to contribute, he didn't notice.

Finally he said, "I think that about covers everything. Any more questions?"

"No, you've been wonderfully clear. I can't wait to get to Paris! It will be so satisfying to know that we'll be helping little children all over the world."

"I'm glad you're joining us," he said warmly.

Sylvie frowned slightly, then asked in a casual tone, "Will Jillian be coming along?"

"No, we have meetings that start early in the morning and often last well into the evening. She'd be alone most of the time. That wouldn't be much fun for her."

"Not since she isn't involved, the way we are.

I'm sure Jillian will keep herself occupied. She has friends of her own here in Venice.''

He gave her a puzzled look. ''I'm not sure who you mean.''

''The handsome young man she was having drinks with in St. Mark's Square. Tina and Isabel saw them there. They would have gone over to say hello, but they didn't want to interrupt. Jillian was having what looked like a very intense conversation with him.''

''And Isabel and Tina told you this, why?'' Gianni asked in a tone that didn't betray any emotion.

Sylvie slanted an uneasy glance at him. ''They just happened to mention it. I guess because they didn't recognize him. You know how we all know each other here. I mean, he isn't one of us.'' She took a deep breath to stop herself from babbling. ''I probably shouldn't have said anything.''

He shrugged. ''It isn't important.''

''That's true. The man might even be somebody she knew from back home. Venice is full of tourists at this time of year.''

''Most of them will be gone soon. High season is almost over.''

''Thank goodness! Well, I'd better run. I've kept you from your shower long enough.'' Sylvie paused at the door. ''I'm sorry I missed Jillian. Say hello for me.''

Gianni remained on the couch, staring at the door for long moments.

Finally he stood and went upstairs.

* * *

Gianni was in his dressing room when Jillian returned to the villa a little later. Assuming that he was still out, she sank down on the couch and put her head back with a sigh.

The thick carpeting muffled his footsteps. Jillian's eyes flew open when he said, "Are you all right?"

"Oh! You startled me. I didn't know you were here."

"I came home some time ago, but I just got around to showering." He was wearing only a pair of slacks. His tanned chest was bare and a towel was slung around his neck. "Is something bothering you?"

"No, of course not!" She smiled brightly. "Why would you think that?"

"The way you're slumped on the couch."

"Shopping is hard work," she joked.

"Even when you don't buy anything? Or are you having your purchases delivered?"

"No, I didn't see anything I liked." She gave him a sharp look. "Why are you giving me the third degree, Gianni? This isn't like you."

"I merely wondered where your packages were. You said you needed some new gowns."

"I do, but nothing really appealed to me. Some days are like that. And the stores are so crowded! It's really difficult to shop."

"All the locals complain, but it doesn't stop them. I suppose your friends shared your annoyance."

Jillian hesitated, wondering whether to tell him about running into Rinaldo that afternoon. Then she decided against it. Why reopen the whole sorry mess? She didn't want to remind Gianni of her immature behavior, way back then.

"I didn't see anybody I knew," she said.

Gianni gazed at her without expression. Finally he said, "Isn't there something you want to tell me, Jillian?"

"I can't think of anything." Her nerves tightened. Could he possibly know about Rinaldo? Why hadn't she told him immediately? Now it was too late. She couldn't pretend she'd forgotten about it.

His face was austere. "I'm sorry you feel you have to lie to me. You're entitled to go wherever you please and see whomever you like. If you've started to feel restless, you could have told me."

"I'm not! I've never been happier. You must know that."

"I thought so, but evidently I was mistaken. You were seen having drinks with a man this afternoon, yet you wanted me to think you spent the day shopping alone. Why, if you're really happy with me?"

"It isn't what you think."

"I don't like what I'm thinking. When we first met I was impressed by your openness, your lack of subterfuge. As we grew closer, you changed my own attitudes. I became less private about my inner feelings. I thought we had a lot to give each other. But a relationship without trust is just an illusion."

Jillian felt like crying, but she bit her lip and

looked directly at him. "I realized as soon as I said I didn't meet anyone today that I should have told you what happened. I ran into Rinaldo."

"*He* was the man you were with?"

"He saw me in a shop and came inside and made a scene. He waved his arms around, shouting that he loved me and wanted me back. Everybody was staring at us and laughing. It was so humiliating! When I couldn't get rid of him, I agreed to go out for coffee. I don't know who saw us, but it wasn't drinks and it wasn't some intimate little bar, if that's what you were told."

"No, she…the person said you were in St. Mark's Square."

"That's right—along with dozens of other people! Rinaldo kept telling me he was sorry. He said he'd make it up to me if I gave him another chance. I told him it was over, that I'd never really loved him in the first place. But of course he didn't believe me. Finally I told him I'd met someone else. He didn't believe that either, but somehow I managed to convince him. I left Rinaldo in the square and came home. That's the whole story, no matter what you heard."

Gianni's taut body had relaxed somewhat, but he was looking at her with a puzzled frown. "Why didn't you tell me this in the first place?"

She sighed. "Because I didn't want you to think I let him manipulate me again. You thought I was a real wimp when we met, and I can't blame you. I was."

"I didn't think that." Gianni smiled reminiscently. "A little naive perhaps, but charming."

"That's a polite way of putting it. I've grown a lot more savvy since then, but I was afraid you'd think he could make me believe he wasn't really a bad person. Or even worse, that I still felt something for him—which couldn't be farther from the truth. All I feel is disgust—and annoyance at myself for not seeing through him."

"As you know, you're not the only one."

"It doesn't make me feel any better to know other women went through what I did. Another reason I didn't tell you was the simplest one of all. I just didn't want to talk about him. It dredges up all the old unpleasantness that I've put out of my mind."

"I suppose that's understandable." Gianni didn't sound fully convinced.

"I'm sorry," Jillian said quietly. "I've never lied to you before. It isn't something I'm good at obviously."

"I didn't enjoy this either." Gianni smiled, warmly this time. "Let's chalk it up to a misunderstanding."

She would have been glad to, but it was difficult to close Pandora's box once it was opened.

Neither of them referred to the incident after that, but there were subtle differences in their relationship. Even though they weren't visible to outsiders.

They were invited to a party on Lido Isle that night, which worked out well. They were both too busy getting dressed to have time for more than a few words of desultory conversation.

Gianni was ready first, so he went downstairs to make sure the ice bucket was filled and hors d'oeuvres had been prepared. Two couples were coming to his villa for a drink first, and then they were all motoring across the canal in his boat.

It was a large party and Jillian knew most of the guests by now. It was normal for Gianni to circulate among his friends instead of staying by her side as he used to, she told herself. He returned often to see that she was among friends, or to ask if she wanted another drink. Anyone else would think he was being sufficiently attentive, but she knew it wasn't the same.

A cold, hard little knot formed in her chest. Had she done irreparable damage to their relationship? If Gianni loved her, he should know she would never betray his trust. If he loved her. The question continued to torment her.

Much later that night when they were back in their bedroom, Jillian felt constrained with Gianni for the first time since their early days together. The easy give-and-take of lovers, secure in their relationship, was missing.

She dawdled in the bathroom, taking longer than usual to brush her teeth and remove her makeup, giving Gianni time to get into bed. Everything would be all right after he took her in his arms, she assured herself.

When she returned to the bedroom all the lights

were out except for the lamp on her nightstand. Gianni was lying on his side with his back to her. Jillian turned off the lamp, slipped between the sheets and waited for him to turn toward her. He didn't move.

She lay motionless, listening to his even breathing. It was possible that he'd fallen asleep while waiting for her, she told herself. Although, Gianni had the energy of three men. He could work all day, play all night and make love until dawn.

Maybe he thought she didn't want to make love tonight. But he could have held her in his arms the way they always went to sleep. There was so little time left, she thought bleakly.

Everything seemed to be back to normal the next day. They had breakfast together and talked about the previous night's party, like a normal married couple. It was a poignant thought that Jillian tried not to dwell on.

Then after breakfast, Gianni wanted some information that she had stored in the computer. He had tried to find it himself without success. They worked together in her office, and she teased him about being computer illiterate.

"I have other talents that make up for it," he said.

"All men have those talents," she laughed.

"I was referring to my athletic ability," he said with mock dignity.

By the time Gianni left for a business meeting, Jillian was reassured.

Her confidence faltered when Sylvie dropped by in the early afternoon.

"I hoped Gianni would be here. We have so many things to discuss. I suppose you know we're going to Paris together," Sylvie said, watching for a reaction.

Jillian didn't oblige. "Yes, I believe he mentioned it, but I didn't pay much attention. I've forgotten when the conference starts."

"A week from today."

"I didn't realize it was that soon," Jillian said slowly. She would have to leave for home a few days after he returned.

"The conference only lasts three days, but I intend to persuade Gianni to spend the rest of the week there. Paris is such a glorious city. It would be foolish to stay for such a short time."

"He might have a different agenda."

"Well, we'll just have to see, won't we?" Sylvie said smugly.

Gianni gave them a wary look when he came home a few minutes later. "I didn't know you were coming," he said to Sylvie. "Have you been here long?"

"Just long enough for Jillian and me to have a little chat. I brought over a proposal I worked up from the data you gave me. Maybe you can look it over. It suggests the places I think should get more attention."

Gianni glanced at the papers she handed him. His interest quickened as his eyes traveled down the first page. "This is very insightful. Come into the den with me. I want to discuss it with you."

Jillian tried not to mind. She knew how passionate Gianni was about his humanitarian work. That was the reason for his interest in Sylvie. It wasn't personal. But they did have a previous relationship, and she would be alone with him for three days in Paris.

Jillian got up from her desk and went out to do some errands. She needed to get away from both of them.

Gianni sensed that Jillian was troubled. Although she tried to hide her feelings, he always knew when something was bothering her. This time, however, he didn't try to get her to talk about it. They were polite to each other and simply skirted the issue.

But when they went to bed that night the irresistible attraction between them couldn't be denied. Gianni reached for her in the darkness and Jillian went into his arms.

"I've missed you," he said in a throaty voice.

"I've been right here," she murmured.

He laughed softly. "I was aware of that, believe me!"

So he *hadn't* been asleep last night! Was he that hurt by her deception? Or was lingering suspicion the reason for his pretense? Even though he said he believed her.

When Gianni's mouth closed over hers, it didn't seem to matter. Their hands moved feverishly, each stroking the other's nude body as though they'd been apart for weeks. Their desire mounted with every suggestive caress, every erotic exploration of moist, hidden places.

When Gianni finally grasped her hips for the ultimate embrace, their lovemaking was even more passionate than usual. Their straining bodies couldn't bear to be apart. They merged over and over again, arching into each other until the final surge of sensation welded them together.

When his breathing returned to normal, Gianni kissed her gently and told her how wonderful she was, how beautiful and exciting. He said she was everything he'd ever wanted in a woman.

But he didn't say he loved her.

Chapter Twelve

Jillian was relieved that she and Gianni had resumed their loving relationship before she had to go home. Leaving him would be the hardest thing she ever had to do, but she couldn't continue to delude herself. Gianni wasn't going to make a commitment. He'd had plenty of time to get over his aversion to the idea. She was just glad they would be parting with only good memories of each other.

Once she'd faced the bitter reality, Jillian tried to put it out of her mind for the brief time they had left. Fortunately her life was too busy for sadness. The nights were crowded with social events, and she spent at least part of every day in the office.

Some days Gianni took her out for lunch, or they

sat in the square, talking over tiny cups of espresso. But this particular day, Gianni had an appointment at his foundation.

He'd only been gone a short time when Marco appeared in the doorway of Jillian's office. "Your eleven o'clock appointment is here, signorina," he announced.

"I don't have an appointment with anyone," she said with a puzzled frown. "Who is it?"

"The gentleman didn't give his name. I asked, but he simply said he was a close friend of yours." The butler's impassive expression changed to disapproval as a man appeared in back of him without waiting to be shown in properly.

"Rinaldo!" Jillian exclaimed, when she saw who it was. "What are you doing here?"

"I thought we should have a little chat," he replied.

"I've told you no, over and over again! What does it take to get rid of you?"

"Shall I escort the gentleman to the door, signorina?" Marco asked.

"I wouldn't advise it," Rinaldo said, looking at Jillian.

She wasn't afraid of his veiled threat, but she didn't want him to make a scene in front of the butler. "Thank you, Marco, but he'll be leaving very shortly. I'll call you if I need you."

They both waited until the man had left, then Jillian said, "How did you know where to find me?"

"I have my ways. I know who your boyfriend is, too, and all about your cozy little setup here. But don't worry, I waited until I saw him leave." He gazed out at the splashing fountain surrounded by a circle of flowers in the carefully tended side garden. "This is one elegant place. I don't blame you for dumping me for the duke. I would have dumped *you* if I'd latched onto somebody this rich."

"That's the first honest thing you ever said to me."

He shrugged. "Why not? I know I won't get you back. I can't compete with the duke's kind of money."

Jillian could have told him he couldn't compete with Gianni on any level, but she didn't want to descend to name calling. "Then why are you here?" she asked.

"I figure you owe me something. I wasted a lot of time on you."

She gasped at the effrontery of the man! "How can you have the nerve to say a thing like that?"

"Let's dispense with the indignation. I don't know how you did it, but you wound up in a palace, and I ended up with *niente*. In all fairness, I think you should share your good fortune with me."

"Why would I do that?" Jillian's nails bit into her palms as she forced herself to remain calm. It wasn't worth the luxury of telling him what a loathsome insect he was. All she wanted to do was get rid of him.

Her tightly leashed anger didn't faze him. "Because if you don't make it worth my while, I'll tell the duke about our affair."

"We didn't have one."

"Do you think he's going to believe that? We spent all of our time together, night and day. The duke is a man of the world. He'll get the picture. And then you'll be out of here so fast you won't have a chance to pack all the goodies I'm sure you conned him into giving you."

"Your threats are meaningless. I already told Gianni all about you, including Maria and the baby. He shares my opinion of you."

"That's because he only heard your side of the story. When I get through telling him my version, how you couldn't keep your hands off me until he came along, he's going to figure you're just interested in what you can get out of him. Especially after I tell him you've been seeing me on the sly all this time." Rinaldo gave her a smug smile. "But it doesn't have to come to that. I'm sure the duke is very generous. A suitable amount of cash, or a nice piece of jewelry could affect my memory."

"For how long? I may have been gullible when we met, but no more. I'm not stupid enough to pay blackmail."

"That's a nasty word. I prefer to think of it as a gift—in appreciation for my tact and understanding."

"You're some piece of work!" She shook her head in disbelief.

"I'm not interested in your opinion of my character. Let's get down to business. I'd prefer cash. How much do you think you can lay your hands on?"

Before she could answer, the telephone rang, startling both of them. It was Gianni.

"I forgot to bring a report I need," he said. "Could you do me a favor and bring it to me here at the foundation?"

"Can I send Marco over with it instead?" Jillian asked. "I had an unexpected visitor this morning. He's here with me now. It's Ri—"

Rinaldo grabbed the phone away from her and put his hand over the mouthpiece. "What the hell do you think you're doing?"

"You wanted to talk to Gianni. Well, now's your chance."

"Don't try to bluff me. If you don't pay up, I swear I'll tell him about us—exactly what I told you! So if you're smart, you'll say your visitor is an old friend—from home maybe. Then get rid of him. Tell him you'll call him back."

When he handed her the phone, Gianni was saying, "Jillian? Why aren't you answering me? What's going on there?"

"Remember Rinaldo? He's here in the office and he has something to say to you."

"Call Marco and have him stay with you until I

get home!'' Gianni ordered. ''I don't want you to be alone with that loathsome con man.''

''You don't have to come home,'' she said. ''I can handle—'' But Gianni had hung up.

''You stupid broad!'' Rinaldo's eyes glittered with rage. ''You just messed things up for both of us. This was the kind of score you dream about.''

''I guess you won't be able to take early retirement after all.''

''That goes for you, too,'' he snarled. ''You think I'll go meekly back to my cheap room and let you continue to live in a palace?'' He flopped into a chair and put his feet on the desk. ''Well, you gambled and lost, baby. I can't wait till the duke gets here. I'm going to enjoy bursting your bubble.''

''You might be due for a disappointment. Gianni hired a detective agency to prepare a report on you. Knowing what they found out, he isn't apt to put much faith in your credibility.''

Rinaldo put his feet on the floor and sat up straight. ''You're lying! Why would the duke go to the trouble of having me investigated?''

''Perhaps because he knows more about human nature than I do. He knew you'd be back.''

''You think you can scare me off, but it won't work. Show me the report—if you have one.''

''It was so sordid that I tore it up.''

''How convenient,'' he sneered. ''So what you're saying is, you don't have any actual proof of my supposed indiscretions.''

"They were a lot more than that. A couple of the women you swindled tried to have you arrested. This isn't the first time you've used blackmail, either. There was that young girl's father who was willing to pay just to get rid of you. You were lucky. If he'd pressed charges, that little 'indiscretion' could have landed you in jail."

Rinaldo's fury mounted as he realized that Jillian knew an alarming amount about his activities. He swore crudely and called her an ugly name, which didn't sound any better in Italian.

"I wouldn't repeat that in front of Gianni when he gets here," she said. "He'd love to have an excuse to vent his displeasure."

"You think you're clever, don't you? You and your millionaire duke! Well, you haven't heard the last of me. I'll get even, no matter how long it takes!" Rinaldo stalked out the door, a little too hurriedly for his threat to be effective.

Jillian realized it was just bluster to save face. He was no match for Gianni, and he knew it.

Her satisfaction dimmed as she waited for Gianni to come home. He was furious at Rinaldo for having the audacity to come into his home. But would Gianni secretly wonder if she'd told him the complete story about her relationship with the other man? It might seem strange that Rinaldo continued to contact her if she'd really told him—in no uncertain terms—that they were through.

Gianni returned in record time, but it seemed an

eternity to Jillian, who continued to stew over the situation. They'd had one misunderstanding over Rinaldo, a serious one. Would this latest incident destroy the trust they'd managed to repair?

She tensed as she heard Gianni's rapid stride in the hallway. He stormed into the office with blazing eyes.

"Where is he?" he demanded after glancing around the room.

"Rinaldo left right after I talked to you."

"What was he doing here in the first place? Why didn't you have Marco throw him out?"

"He would only have come back," she said quietly. "Rinaldo came here to blackmail me."

She told him all the things Rinaldo had threatened. Then she waited for his reaction. It would break her heart if Gianni doubted her. But she would have to live with it. The only lie she'd ever told him might be her undoing.

"You thought there was a chance I would believe him?" He looked at her impassively, which gave her no clue.

"Rinaldo can be very convincing. It's what he does for a living."

"Would you have believed him if he told you damaging stories about *me?*"

"No, that's different. You've never given me any reason to doubt you."

"And you think I would let that poor excuse for a man shake my faith in *you?* Because of one misunderstanding? You are so wrong! I've never known anyone as sincere and guileless as you. *Cara mia,* I would trust you with my life.''

Tears misted her eyes. She should have known Gianni wouldn't disappoint her. He never had.

Taking her in his arms, he smoothed her hair gently. ''I'm just sorry you had to deal with that cretin alone. I want to take care of you and make your life beautiful.''

''You have, darling.'' She lifted her face, smiling through her tears.

The kiss they exchanged was exquisitely tender.

Rinaldo would have been furious to know that he'd brought Jillian and Gianni closer together, rather than destroying their relationship. They were supremely happy. Only one thing bothered her slightly.

Gianni avoided any mention of his trip to Paris until a couple of days before he was due to leave. She thought it was odd that he wouldn't discuss little details of the upcoming conference with her. Especially since he was so enthusiastic about the work he'd be doing.

Did he think she'd pout because he didn't ask her to go along? Jillian *was* secretly hurt that Gianni didn't invite her, and not because she was jealous of the time he'd be spending with Sylvie.

She would simply have enjoyed being in Paris with him, no matter how much or how little time they could spend together. But she had no intention of telling him that. An invitation had to be given freely, or not at all.

Gianni finally got around to the subject of his trip when they were in bed together. What better place? Jillian thought, a little cynically. Any problems they had, always dissolved when they were in each other's arms.

"I'm going to miss holding you like this, even if it's just for a few nights," he said, fitting her body more closely to his. "I'll be leaving early Wednesday morning for the conference."

"I thought you were just going to leave me a note on the pillow, saying goodbye." Jillian couldn't resist the barb, although she'd kept her voice light.

He slanted a wary glance at her. "I would have asked you to go if I thought you'd enjoy yourself."

"It's all right. There are still some things I'd like to do around here before I leave. Touristy things that wouldn't interest you. I'll have a chance to do them while you're gone."

"What do you mean, before you leave?" He frowned. "Where are you going?"

"Summer vacation is almost over. I have to go back to work."

"It's only August! Surely school doesn't start this soon."

"It's the end of August, and teachers have to report in earlier for meetings, and to organize our curriculum for the semester."

"When are you planning to leave?"

"A few days after you get home. That reminds me. I'd better make my plane reservation." She'd been putting it off, hoping for a miracle.

"Do you really have to go back?" he asked slowly. "You could stay here and apply for a work permit."

Jillian stopped believing in fairy-tale endings. "And then what kind of a job could I get? I really enjoy my work at home, and in a few years I'll have tenure. It's always nice to know you can't be fired arbitrarily." Her joking tone masked the pain.

"I can't even remember what life was like without you."

She could have told him it would all come back to him. It was like riding a bicycle; you don't forget. But she didn't want the short time they had left to be marred by bitterness. Since this was all there would ever be, she intended to make every moment a shining one.

Putting her arms around his neck, she whispered, "Don't think about tomorrow. Make love to me tonight."

His ardent kiss made time stand still for both of them.

Gianni was preoccupied the next day. Jillian wished she could believe he was mulling over ways to keep her in Venice. But there was only one way. Could he be considering it? That would account for his solemn expression. The idea of marriage always spooked him. She laughed breathlessly at this ray of hope.

Gianni's sister stopped by in the late afternoon. It was a warm day and Jillian had her office windows open to take advantage of the breeze from the garden. Gianni was working outside. At least, he had some papers spread out on the patio table. Much of the time he spent just staring at the sea gulls wheeling overhead.

Marco brought Angelina outside to the garden.

Jillian could hear their voices, but she didn't want to close the window and lose the cool breeze. It wasn't as if she was eavesdropping. Gianni knew she was here.

He made an effort to be pleasant to his sister, hoping to avoid an argument, for once. ''Where are the boys? I haven't seen them in almost a week.''

''Their nanny took them to soccer practice. I wanted to talk to you alone, Gianni.''

He stifled a sigh. ''Of course. What can I do for you?''

''You can talk some sense into that so-called husband of mine!''

''What has he done now?''

''What I've suspected him of all along, but this time I'm sure of it. He's having an affair with some floozy. And don't tell me I'm imagining things. I have proof! He told me he had to work late, but when I called him at the office he wasn't there.''

"You're overreacting as usual, Angelina. Maybe he walked down the hall and didn't hear the phone. Or maybe he went to the men's room. There could be any number of reasons for his not being in the office when you called."

"Don't bother making excuses for him. I know when my own husband is having an affair. He hasn't wanted to make love to me for weeks. Doesn't that tell you something?"

"A man finds it hard to get romantic over a woman who is constantly accusing him of something," Gianni drawled.

"That's right, take his side. You men are all alike!"

Their argument escalated with both of them getting angrier by the minute.

Jillian wanted to close the window, but it was too late now. She didn't want to embarrass them by calling attention to herself.

Finally Gianni threw up his hands. "I give up! Maybe you should divorce him and put an end to this bitterness. It couldn't be any worse than trying to preserve a marriage that's already dead."

Angelina burst into tears. "I'll never divorce Rudolfo! He's the father of my children."

Gianni's stormy face softened. "They might be better off. It isn't healthy for them to hear you two wrangling constantly. You could get counseling from the church," he said tentatively. "There are ways to handle a situation like this."

"How can you even suggest such a thing? I love Rudolfo. I've never wanted anyone else. I'll die if he leaves me!"

"Stop being so dramatic. You and Rudolfo have been battling for years. You'd be better off at least filing for a formal separation. Then you could both get on with your lives."

"I don't *have* a life without him. You don't understand because you've never loved anyone so completely that you're only half alive without them. Father was like that after Mother died. I understand him now because I'm like him. You're not."

"You think it's a good thing to be that emotionally dependent on another person?"

Jillian could imagine the harsh lines in his face.

"At least you'd know what true love is."

"You're saying I'm not capable of love?"

"Not the kind where you're able to commit completely," Angelina replied.

She was surprisingly insightful, Jillian thought sadly. She pushed her chair back quietly and left the room, not wanting to hear any more.

Gianni left the house shortly after his sister did. He didn't tell anyone where he was going. When he got home much later, he was quiet and withdrawn.

Jillian avoided him as much as possible. He didn't seem to mind, or even notice. She could only hope his annoyance with Angelina wouldn't last too long. He was leaving for Paris in a matter of days.

The night before Gianni left was satisfyingly ro-

mantic. They made love until dawn, even though
Jillian reminded him that he had an early morning
flight and a full day ahead.

"I can sleep anytime," he answered. "I won't be
able to make love to you for three days."

She couldn't argue with that logic. Or, more accurately, she didn't want to.

It felt strange to be without Gianni. Jillian was so
used to waking up beside him, to discussing the
day's news at breakfast, all the little things they did
together throughout the day.

Get used to it, she told herself. This is the way
it's going to be. When the thought became unbear-
able she went out and wandered around Venice.

The fabled city succeeded in cheering her up for
hours at a time. She took a vaporetto to the Island
of Burano and watched elderly women make exquisite lace by hand, weaving delicate threads into in-
tricate patterns. The handkerchiefs they made were
so lovely that Jillian bought a selection to give to
all her friends at home.

The museums of Venice kept her occupied for
hours at a time. There were so many of them. The
art work filled palaces and more modest galleries.
When she couldn't absorb any more, she went shopping in the stalls at either end of the Rialto Bridge
and bought scarves and sweaters to take home as
gifts for her family.

She stayed out for dinner one night, too, dining

at an outdoor restaurant on a cobblestone square. That wasn't a success, though. The tables were filled with young couples gazing into each other's eyes and holding hands.

Gianni telephoned several times, but their conversations were unsatisfactory. There were usually other people around, and he always sounded distracted.

"I just wanted to see if you were all right," he said one day, after they'd only spoken for a couple of minutes.

"I'm fine. Are you having a good time?" she asked, to keep him on the line longer.

"I wouldn't put it that way. I didn't come here to have fun. We're getting a lot accomplished, which is very gratifying."

"That's what I meant."

"Well, I'm due at a meeting. I really have to go. I'll try to call you later tonight."

"You don't have to do that. I can tell you're preoccupied with the conference."

"I told you I was going to be busy every minute," he said, with a hint of impatience. "Now you know why I didn't ask you to come. I miss you, *cara.*" His voice finally deepened to the note she was looking for.

"I miss you, too. Don't let Sylvie talk you into staying over the weekend," Jillian said, in what she hoped was a light tone.

"Count on it! Now I really must run, darling. My meeting is due to start momentarily."

Jillian hung up with a sigh.

She was surprised when Gianni's sister showed up a short time later. But she was at such loose ends that even Angelina's company was welcome.

The other woman looked radiant—which was unusual. She normally wore one of three expressions: petulant, tearful or angry.

"You look cheerful today," Jillian remarked cautiously.

"That doesn't begin to describe how I feel! Do you have Gianni's telephone number in Paris? I want to talk to him."

"I can tell you where he's staying, but he's rather hard to reach. He'll be home tomorrow night, though."

"I won't be here. Rudolfo and I are going away on a second honeymoon."

"Really? I mean…how lovely."

Angelina laughed at the look on Jillian's face. "I don't blame you for being surprised. All you've ever heard me do is complain about my husband. Our marriage has been in trouble for a long time, but I refused to believe Gianni when he said I was as much to blame as Rudolfo."

"I suppose it's hard to recognize your own faults."

"Exactly! I was on the verge of a separation. In fact, Gianni said that's what I should do."

"Your brother isn't exactly qualified to be a marriage counselor."

"That's what I thought. But he could tell I didn't really want to leave Rudolfo. By giving me his blessing he made me face reality. When I started to think about what my life would be like, he told me to sit down with Rudolfo and tell him—calmly for once—how perilously close we were to splitting up."

That must have been after she left the office, Jillian thought.

"I took Gianni's advice because it was my only option. When Rudolfo realized that I was willing to listen to his grievances, we talked about all the things that were causing problems between us. It was as if the years rolled back and we were young lovers again. My wonderful brother saved our marriage!"

That was pretty ironic, Jillian thought after Angelina had left, considering how Gianni felt about marriage. To be fair, their example might make anyone think twice. His sister and brother-in-law weren't exactly poster children for the institution.

Would it change his opinion to see that problems could be worked out if two people loved each other? Perhaps, but it was too late for Gianni and her.

Jillian could barely wait for Gianni to return the next night. She had washed her hair and brushed it till it shone like wine-colored satin flowing around her shoulders. He liked it loose and natural. She had also selected his favorite gown—a long, lace-trimmed caftan in a shade of blue the color of her eyes.

She was waiting for him in their suite, sitting on the couch and trying without much success to read a book. A bottle of champagne was cooling in a silver ice bucket, and some crystal bowls on the coffee table held little snacks, although Gianni would already have had dinner.

When he finally arrived, their reunion was satisfyingly ardent. Gianni held her tightly in his arms, running his fingers through her carefully brushed hair and kissing her with deep emotion.

"I feel as if I've been gone for weeks instead of days," he said with a groan of pleasure.

"I thought it was at least a month." Jillian stroked his cheek. "But I can't complain since it was for such a good cause. Was the conference a success?"

"Yes, we accomplished a lot this time."

They sat on the couch and Gianni told her how they'd cut through seemingly miles of infuriating red tape, so hungry children in trouble spots around the globe would get the immediate help they needed.

"I'm proud of you," she said softly.

"I'm only one participant. Everybody there was working toward a common goal. They're dedicated people."

"I must admit I was surprised that Sylvie is part

of your group. It's not the sort of thing I'd expect her to be interested in." Jillian tried to sound judicious, rather than catty. What she really wanted to know was how much time they'd spent together.

"This was Sylvie's first meeting," he said briefly.

"So I suppose you had to show her the ropes."

"I didn't have time. I barely saw her."

"Not *too* barely I hope," Jillian said with a little laugh.

Gianni gave her a sharp look. "Don't you trust me?"

She gazed back at him, hiding her apprehension. *Did* something happen between him and Sylvie in Paris? "You're being remarkably defensive," she said lightly. "It was supposed to be a joke."

"I'm sorry, darling. There were a lot of heated discussions at the conference, and I guess I'm still wound up. But it's no excuse for taking that tone with you."

"I understand," she said, not willing to mar his homecoming with an argument.

"Let's have some champagne to celebrate our reunion. It was very thoughtful of you to have it chilling." He lifted the bottle out of the ice bucket and twisted the cork.

"I have all sorts of hidden talents," she joked.

"Not hidden from me." He kissed her sensuously before pouring the champagne into two stemmed glasses.

As they were gazing into each other's eyes, there

was a knock on the bedroom door, surprising both of them. No one ever bothered them here.

Marco was at the door, looking apologetic. "I am sorry to disturb you, signore, but the Countess of Rivoli is here to see you."

Gianni's frown deepened to a scowl. "Tell her I'll speak to her tomorrow."

"I told her you were—"

The butler's words were cut off by Sylvie, who pushed by him into the room. "I thought I'd save you the trouble of coming downstairs," she said.

"What are you doing here?" Gianni demanded.

"That's not very polite. What happened to that famous charm of yours?"

"I exhausted it in Paris—along with my patience."

"This isn't like you, darling." She glanced at Jillian, then back at him with a knowing expression. "Oh, now I understand."

"I don't know what you think you're going to accomplish by this," he said through clenched teeth.

Instead of answering his question, she said, "Is that champagne? How nice. Aren't you going to offer me a glass?" When he didn't move, she said, "Never mind, I can pour it myself. Did Gianni tell you what an exciting time we had in Paris?" she asked Jillian as she strolled across the room.

"He said the trip was very successful."

"Yes, I suppose that would describe it," Sylvie laughed.

Gianni's face was formidable. "How long is this going to go on?" he asked.

"I'm sorry, my love. You must be exhausted after getting so little sleep the last few nights. I just came to return your ring." She took a man's heavy gold signet ring out of her purse. "You left it on the nightstand in my room last night. I know how much it means to you, and I didn't want you to think you'd lost it." She looked from him to Jillian with a smug expression. "Well, I'm sure you two have a lot to talk about. Don't bother to see me out."

Gianni and Jillian remained motionless in the silent room after she left, like figures in a wax museum. Finally he broke the spell.

"I suppose you're convinced that I had a passionate affair with Sylvie in Paris."

"It wouldn't have taken any effort on your part. We both know that's the only reason she wanted to be a delegate."

"How could you know that when I didn't?"

"Because women can tell when another woman is a phoney and men can't. Honestly, Gianni! I'll never understand how you could be attracted to that woman."

"I've tried to tell you there was never anything serious between us."

"That obviously wasn't the way *she* felt."

Deep lines were grooved around his mouth. "I won't try to convince you that nothing happened between us at the conference. Why should you believe me when all the evidence points the other way?''

Jillian smiled as her annoyance at the other woman dissipated. "I can think of one reason. You've always been honest with me."

Incredulous hope dawned in his eyes. "You trust me? Just because I say I'm telling the truth?"

"Isn't that what trust means?"

"Darling Jillian." He took her hand and brought it to his lips. "I don't deserve you."

"That's very possible," she said mischievously. "But not because of any hanky-panky with Sylvie. It was so obvious that she came here to cause trouble between us. How stupid does she think I am?"

"You're a wonderful, wise woman. Let me tell you what really happened."

"You don't have to."

"I want to, darling."

"All right, but I can guess just about everything except how she got the ring. Did she steal it somehow?" The gold ring was a family heirloom. It bore the di Destino crest. Jillian knew Gianni would never give it to the woman.

"It was a little more complicated than that. I always knew Sylvie was a bit shallow, but I honestly thought she shared my interest in the children's fund. She showed me independent studies she'd made on her own initiative. I was impressed."

"You can bet she paid somebody to research and write them for her."

''No doubt. When we got to Paris, Sylvie pretty much gave up the pretense of being interested in the conference. She tried to get me to skip the meetings and take her out partying. When I refused, she suggested dinner after the meetings, or a late supper. I refused those invitations as well, and she finally seemed to get the message. I should have realized she wasn't the sort to give up that easily.''

''How *did* she get you alone?''

''It was last night, the final night of the conference. She left a message, asking me to come to her room. The message said she'd heard something alarming that I should know about. It concerned one of our fund-raisers. If my mind hadn't been so occupied with important matters, I would have realized it was unlikely that she'd have inside information of any sort,'' Gianni said with chagrin.

''You couldn't know for sure,'' Jillian said, while privately marveling at how inventive a really determined woman could be.

''When I got to her room, Sylvie was nude under a revealing negligee that was only partially closed. The bed was turned down and there was a bottle of scotch and two glasses on the dresser.''

How tacky could the woman get? All that was missing was strip tease music and scented body oil for massages, Jillian thought derisively. But she remained silent.

''I told her as kindly as possible that this was a mistake,'' Gianni continued. ''But she refused to ac-

cept that. She began talking wildly, saying she loved
me, insisting that we belonged together. I finally realized she wasn't going to listen to reason. I started
to leave, but she threw her arms around my neck
and hung on like a leech. When I tried to pull her
arms away, my ring got caught in one of the long,
dangling earrings she was wearing.''

"Well, at least her ears weren't naked.'' Jillian
grinned.

"It wasn't a joke! I couldn't untangle the ring
without damaging her earlobe, so I just slipped the
ring off my finger and left. Sylvie came here tonight
to get even for being rejected.''

"It could have been worse,'' Jillian teased. "You
did get your ring back.''

"You're not upset? You really mean it?''

"You're upset enough for both of us.'' She un-
fastened the top buttons of his shirt. "We've spent
enough time talking about that tiresome woman.
Let's make love.''

To her surprise, Gianni said, "First we have to
finish our talk—and I want to give you something I
bought for you in Paris.'' He reached in his pocket
and brought out a small, square velvet box.

When she opened it, Jillian's breath caught in her
throat. Inside, on a bed of white satin was an exquisite ruby ring. The large center stone was surrounded by sparkling diamonds. Was it the engagement ring she wanted more than anything in the

world—or just another of Gianni's expensive gifts? She gazed at him uncertainly.

"Will you marry me, my love?" he asked, answering her unspoken question in the most satisfactory way. "I wouldn't blame you if you said no, after the way I've treated you."

"How can you say that? You've been wonderful to me."

"You're very forgiving." He paused to smooth her hair gently. "I've been in love with you almost from the day we met, but I wouldn't admit it to myself. I never wanted anyone to have the power over me that you do."

She nodded. "I guessed that. Why did you change your mind—about me, about marriage?"

"When you told me you were leaving, I was devastated. Although I felt that you would stay if I asked you to marry me, I'd been so adamantly opposed to the idea of marriage for so long that I couldn't seem to say the words. Maybe I was hoping you would suggest it, and then I'd be forced to make up my mind. I would never have let you go."

"But the decision had to be yours. If I'd coerced you into marrying me, you would have resented me for it, sooner or later," Jillian said. "You had to want it as much as I did."

"That's exactly right. You're a very wise lady."

"I didn't think it would ever happen after you had that argument with your sister."

"I was angry because I knew some of the things

she said were true. It wasn't a sudden revelation. I *had* avoided commitment all my life because I didn't want to be emotionally dependent on another person. But she was wrong about my capacity to love. I thought about you constantly in Paris, about how meaningless my life would be without you. And suddenly I realized that didn't scare me anymore. I had finally learned what it means to love someone completely, without holding anything back.''

He took her hands and raised them to his lips. ''Please say you'll marry me, Jillian. I love you more than any man has ever loved a woman.''

Tears dampened her long lashes as the impossible dream came true. ''I never thought I'd hear you say it. I'd given up hope.''

''Don't ever give up on me, *mi amore*. I couldn't survive without you.''

''You'll never have to,'' she said, clasping her arms around his neck.

Gianni's tender kiss was filled with love and the promise of a lifelong partnership. Their pretend engagement would soon be a real marriage.

* * * * *

ATTENTION
LINDSAY McKENNA FANS!

Morgan's men are made for battle—
but are they ready for love?

Coming in February 2001:

MAN WITH A MISSION
(Silhouette Special Edition #1376)

Featuring rugged army ranger Jake Travers as
he comes under the captivating command of
beautiful Captain Ana Lucia Cortina.

*And available in March 2001,
a brand-new, longer-length single title:*

Morgan's Mercenaries:
Heart of Stone

Featuring Captain Maya Stevenson as she is reunited
with Major Dane York—her powerful enemy
turned passionate lover!

And in April 2001, look for a special collection
featuring the stories that started it all—
Morgan's Mercenaries: *In the Beginning....*

Available at your favorite retail outlet.

Where love comes alive™

#1 *New York Times* bestselling author

NORA ROBERTS

brings you more of the loyal and loving,
tempestuous and tantalizing Stanislaski family.

Coming in February 2001

The Stanislaski Sisters

Natasha and Rachel

Though raised in the Old World traditions of their
family, fiery Natasha Stanislaski and cool, classy
Rachel Stanislaski are ready for a *new* world of love....

*And also available in February 2001 from
Silhouette Special Edition, the newest book in the
heartwarming Stanislaski saga*

CONSIDERING KATE

Natasha and Spencer Kimball's daughter Kate turns her
back on old dreams and returns to her hometown, where
she finds the *man* of her dreams.

Available at your favorite retail outlet.

Where love comes alive™

THE
BABY BET

Joan Elliott Pickart

continues her popular miniseries
Silhouette Special Edition in February 2001
when MacAllister friends find
love and laughter!

HER LITTLE SECRET, SE #1377
Eligible sheriff Cable Montana wasn't looking to remarry,
but the town's matchmakers determined that lovely
Lindsey Patterson would make him a wonderful wife.
Shockingly, Cable's rock-hard resistance to love
shattered when he was with Lindsey, but a
little secret stood between them and any
future together....

And don't miss
THE BABY BET: PARTY OF THREE,
on sale August 2001,
another big-book installment of
THE BABY BET!

Available at your favorite retail outlet.

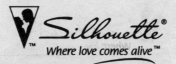
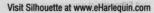

Silhouette invites you to come back to Whitehorn, Montana...

MONTANA MAVERICKS

WED IN WHITEHORN—
12 BRAND-NEW stories that capture living and loving beneath the Big Sky where legends live on and love lasts forever!

MM

And the adventure continues...

February 2001—
Jennifer Mikels *Rich, Rugged...Ruthless* (#9)

March 2001—
Cheryl St.John *The Magnificent Seven* (#10)

April 2001—
Laurie Paige *Outlaw Marriage* (#11)

May 2001—
Linda Turner *Nighthawk's Child* (#12)

Available at your favorite retail outlet.

Silhouette®
Where love comes alive™

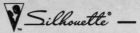

Silhouette® —

where love comes alive—online...

eHARLEQUIN.com

your romantic escapes

— Indulgences —
♥ Monthly guides to indulging yourself,
such as:
★ Tub Time: A guide for bathing beauties
★ Magic Massages: A treat for tired feet

— Horoscopes —
♥ Find your daily Passionscope, weekly
Lovescopes and Erotiscopes

♥ Try our compatibility game

— Reel Love —
♥ Read all the latest romantic
movie reviews

— Royal Romance —
♥ Get the latest scoop on your favorite
royal romances

— Romantic Travel —
♥ For the most romantic destinations, hotels
and travel activities

If you enjoyed what you just read,
then we've got an offer you can't resist!

Take 2 bestselling
love stories FREE!
Plus get a FREE surprise gift!

Clip this page and mail it to Silhouette Reader Service™

IN U.S.A.	IN CANADA
3010 Walden Ave.	P.O. Box 609
P.O. Box 1867	Fort Erie, Ontario
Buffalo, N.Y. 14240-1867	L2A 5X3

YES! Please send me 2 free Silhouette Special Edition® novels and my free surprise gift. Then send me 6 brand-new novels every month, which I will receive months before they're available in stores. In the U.S.A., bill me at the bargain price of $3.80 plus 25¢ delivery per book and applicable sales tax, if any*. In Canada, bill me at the bargain price of $4.21 plus 25¢ delivery per book and applicable taxes**. That's the complete price and a savings of at least 10% off the cover prices—what a great deal! I understand that accepting the 2 free books and gift places me under no obligation ever to buy any books. I can always return a shipment and cancel at any time. Even if I never buy another book from Silhouette, the 2 free books and gift are mine to keep forever. So why not take us up on our invitation. You'll be glad you did!

235 SEN C224
335 SEN C225

Name	(PLEASE PRINT)	
Address	Apt.#	
City	State/Prov.	Zip/Postal Code

* Terms and prices subject to change without notice. Sales tax applicable in N.Y.
** Canadian residents will be charged applicable provincial taxes and GST.
  All orders subject to approval. Offer limited to one per household.
  ® are registered trademarks of Harlequin Enterprises Limited.

SPED00   ©1998 Harlequin Enterprises Limited

In March 2001,

Silhouette Desire

presents the next book in

DIANA PALMER's

enthralling *Soldiers of Fortune* trilogy:

THE WINTER SOLDIER

Cy Parks had a reputation around Jacobsville for his taciturn and solitary ways. But spirited Lisa Monroe wasn't put off by the mesmerizing mercenary, and drove him to distraction with her sweetly tantalizing kisses. Though he'd never admit it, Cy was getting mighty possessive of the enchanting woman who needed the type of safeguarding only he could provide. But who would protect the beguiling beauty from *him…?*

Soldiers of Fortune…prisoners of love.

Silhouette®

Where love comes alive™

Available only from Silhouette Desire at your favorite retail outlet.

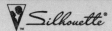